T0103823

What's Opposite of Two
"A Lonely Me and a Lonely You"

What's Opposite of Two
"A Lonely Me and a Lonely You"

Satyam Swaroop

PARTRIDGE

To order additional copies of this book, contact
Partridge India
000 800 10062 62
orders.india@partridgepublishing.com

www.partridgepublishing.com/india

Contents

This book is dedicated to

Acknowledgement

Writing a thanking note for this book was really a tough job for me. This book needed lots of endeavour by different people in its assembling. Let's go ahead and thank those people who made this book wonderful.

I was interested in the writing sector but never thought of getting it published but 'Sneha' one of my close friend came to me and asked me to pen down my feelings and get it published. She provided me with the first step towards my write up 'The Title'. Heartiest thanks to her contribution.

My parents were always standing behind me in every respect, they were like the pillars of my book, and especially my father who worked every single minute with me to get this book published, without him I was not able to achieve this height. All credits goes to him.

Nishant, Sandip, Rohit, Praveen, Ismail, Uday, Shubhang, Shubham, Jakhar, Punit, Vaibhav, Umar, Gehlot, Dev and Vikas they were always standing at my back to assist me in every respect. They all the time used to snoop to my quotes and write up. Thanks to all of them for being such an excellent listener.

Special thanks to Amit Mahawar who provide me with ample of his time in picturing my book during my writing period. His own Hawk Eye photography page on Facebook helped me in creating my cover designs. Thanks to him for clicking my picture and getting it to a professional look. Thanks to Praveen sir who helped me in editing this paperback.

Last but not the least heartily thanks to my PSA Gemma Ramos who provided me with lot of extensions in my publishing and helped me a lot in every respect.

Chapter 1

Parentage on own

Happy faces all around the house, reason my cousin's marriage had to be systematized in a week. All the preparations were going on a high note. At that time I was worried about further proceedings of my career, reason my institution had alarmed the bell for me that I can't carry out my academic session there anymore. I was tensed so were my parents.

Marriage took its place at a very happy note, now the entire family had been left with a single task to make me a gentleman. All of them kept busy suggesting me what to do or what not to do in my life after my secondary education. I was like a 'lamb' which was going to be cut and people were busy making it cut properly. I hate those instants.

I studied in a reputed school of the town and after my primary education was over I shifted my room to my aunt's place in BIHAR. It was a place full of greenery and awesome weather. You can't sleep without blankets there, I loved the atmosphere of the town, silence was there, and people mind their own business. My aunt lived in a place which people called a Porsche area. All time electricity, water, and many more amenities were being provided in that area. I know water, electricity had been the most common amenities provided, but, the state in which I used to live was behind in all these resources. Government wants to fulfill their issues first later on they will provide us with the basic amenities.

The place where I used to live was like heaven on the earth. I loved the interiors, as well as the old galleries present in the house. People who lived there loved me a lot whatever I asked for got fulfilled without any queries. This was the first time I was living without my parents, and at the start it was like fun living without your parents, no restriction, no guardianship, whatever will happen must be under your copyright. A free life had begun for me. But when it comes back to the memories of home, then there is no synonym of my sweet home. Whatever the restriction had been imposed on you, from outside you are unhappy but from inside you are a happy man. My second crucial academic stage was on top of my head. I always hate study. My mindset was that people must have lots of co-curricular skills inside him to provide them with the capacity to fight through any situations. But these thought were limited to my mind only, I don't had this much dare inside me to talk to my parents about this. Speaking to my parents about my hobbies would make them low so I kept myself silent always.

I started my secondary education happily. Daily routine was like a torture and boring. 7'o clock to the school, 3'o clock back to home, tuitions, and life was running on a single track system, nothing could come in between me and my routine before the weekends. After passing couple of months things got settled. Life started picking up its gear I had adjusted myself with this environment. I always had interest in co- curricular activities. I loved participating in extra activities. I loved singing, playing basketball was my passion.

A farewell party had to be organized in our school and I was one of the core committee members for that event. Time was being passed in those preparations, as the school had provided us with a short period of time for the function to be carried out. While I was practicing my song, a member from the core committee came to me and greeted me 'HIII'.

She was Simran. Tall height, long curly hairs, and broad eyes, she was like a perfect piece of beauty made in a relaxed way by the almighty. I got stunned why she approached me?

Somehow I managed to answer my inside questions and greeted her with a broken h-e-l-l-o. Guys like me had always the hesitation inside them how to interact with a girl.

"You had a good voice; I liked the way you sing" – she said smiling.

"No, it's not like that I just love to sing that's the reason I used to sing" – I added.

"Never seen you before in the school, new admission" – she asked.

"Yup, I had my admission this year only. I had my primary education in my town and I'm here for my secondary's."- I said

"My father is about to come. I have to go. Bye see you later"- she said.

I was a happy guy from inside because a lot of things had happened with me within few hours. I went home taking a smile back onto my face. Days were passing happily we used to spend time together in the school. I was a regular student and all credits goes to her for my strong attendance.

The Farewell was about to be held within two days and we all were practicing for our tasks.

Farewell was awesome, all the teachers were happy with our management. After the farewell I was standing near the stage, Simran came to me and asked me to meet her near the fee office after the final bell.

I was shocked what she said but the truth was that I had got what I wanted. After the final bell I rushed away from my class and reached the place where she was about to come, after fifteen minutes she arrived.

She was looking here and there as if she was searching for me but she was in a different mood that day. She handed me a sheet of paper as if it was an accident and she asked me to reply back and she went running out of the gate.

I somehow controlled my patience and put that sheet in my pocket and marched towards my home. Today the distance between school and home was the smallest one. I was rushing towards my home in a hurry to read that that sheet of paper. I can't wait for that paper to reveal its story. I wasn't able to had control on my feelings to open that chit and read it what had been written inside it, but I kept my serenity within my body and reached home.

Without having lunch, without changing my uniform I was on my bed handling that sheet of paper and a smile on my face, I opened it and I was shocked after seeing the numbers written inside that sheet, it was her contact number and a note "waiting for you to call".

I was in a matter of thinking "I saw her beautiful face, her behavior, and her intelligence of doing work, so I had a little crush on her but what did she saw in me"?? Thinking all these when my eyes flipped I didn't knew.

"Vicky! Vicky!" – It was my sister waking me up for my tuitions but I was lost in a different world, somehow she woke me up

"Why didn't you have your lunch today"—she asked

I had been exhausted in my school these days due to the workload and all other stuffs, when I slept didn't remembered – I said

Anyhow I dressed myself for the tuition and left.

Chapter 2

Sweet 16!!!

"Hello"- a sweet voice from the other side, it was her, I was lost in her voice.

Another "hello" – she was louder this time.

H-E-L-L-O – I said with a breaking voice.

"I was waiting for your call"- she said

"Did you recognize my voice?" – I confirmed

"Yes I do recognize your voice" – she was smiling at my silly questions.

"Why did you gave me your contact number?" – I asked

Another silly question from my side. Thanks to the almighty he was playing games with my conversation.

"My dad is home talk to you later. Bye" – she cut the call and left me with a disguise.

These all were the part of attraction we both had on each other. At this stage we all had these feelings when we were on the edge of diversion between our studies and the so called 'love'. It happened to all @16.

"Yes I was at my 16, lots of attractions, lots of deviations was taking place in my life. At this stage our mind doesn't comes under our control, it goes with the flow. So was I going on with the flow and enjoying my life".

We daily hang out together, late night calls and chats had become a schedule to my life. We both were enjoying these moments. One night while talking I asked her

"Do you have any boyfriend?" – It felt embarrassed but I asked her

"No I had earlier but I have no boyfriend at this present time"

We promised each other to keep this friendship simple and sober. She agreed without any hesitation, she also wanted this to happen. But we all know no relationship was there around us which we could call 'perfect'. We both were happy at our ends. She wanted to talk to me and pass her time and I wanted a girl like her to hang out with and get people burnt with her beauty. We both were fulfilling each other's demand.

In our city "CHATH" was one of the most celebrated festivals, I had always celebrated this auspicious festival at my grandmother's home, but that time I wasn't at my grandmother's home. My mom was here at my uncle's place to celebrate this festival. My uncle's son had also come on his first vacation after the joining of engineering college in Mysore.

At that time, going to an engineering college was like you are the god and the whole world is going to worship you for what you have done. I and my cousin were best buddies at a time; we used to have all our stuffs together. During vacations whenever we met we had a blast, how our vacations passed we didn't know. But time changes so do people, we had a simple handshake and a formal hello. I was shocked after seeing the reaction of my cousin.

"Time changes people, time changes everything". I murmured inside me.

Anyway we celebrated the festival with lots of joy and happiness as we celebrated it at our home. I was sitting in the hall listening to the chit chats of my family members that was the only time when the reunion of the family members took place. Enjoying with my family members was one of the best parts of my life. They kept discussing their endless topics and enjoying their leisure time.

Suddenly my cousin phone rang, as he was not there at that time my aunt asked me to take that call. I picked the call

"Hello" – a heart melting voice came from that side I was lost in that girl's voice.

"Bhaiya is not at home, could you call after sometime. I will let him know that you have called"- I said.

"Tell him that VINNI had called"- she said and greeted me bye.

I thought it might be my cousin's girlfriend. I enquired but she was just a friend of him. Her voice was beautiful, seemed like a group of violin had been played in my ear. I wanted to listen her once again so I took her cell number from my cousin's cell and copied it in mine without letting him know. I knew that was wrong but her voice made me do so, her voice had got something some sort of attractive powers. I thought so.

All the functions were over; I was again on the same path following my daily routines. School and tuitions had become a mess for me. I was neither serious for my studies nor any other activities seek my interest, I had lost all the interest in my life due to that hectic time table of mine. I stopped texting Simran, didn't respond to her calls, life was taking me to other path apart from that boring schedule. I was happy in me, enjoyed my leisure time hanging out with friends and playing games.

One day as I was sitting idle in my room playing with my cell phone, suddenly I saw an unsaved number in it. I had no idea whose number was that, I thought hard but it was out of my mind, finally, I decided to check that number, I called on that number. Nobody picked the call, I thought it would be disturbing for the person whom I have called, so I didn't called back. As I was busy in listening to my favorite collections, my phone beeped. I checked that number and was wondering where had I saw that number, suddenly, it clicked my mind, this was the number I was trying to find out whom it belonged to, I picked up the call.

"Hello!! Who is this?"- Same voice which I had heard a couple of months ago and I was flattered again.

"This is Vicky"- I said

"Do you know me, actually you guys don't have any work to do and so you start dialing different pattern numbers"- she shouted at me.

"I do know you by your voice and I haven't dialed a random number this number was there in my contact but without name that's why I dialed it to check who was on the other side, but you accused me earlier"- I said her

"How could you know me by my voice"? She asked.

"We had talked earlier, I'm Akshay's younger brother who spoke to you on behalf of my brother."- I said

"Oh I see, you must have illustrated this earlier as I smashed you with my words without any reason, I'm so sorry" - she said calmly

"How did you save my contact, I called at your brother's cell"- she was at the point

"Yes didi I'm coming" – I said and cut the call

No one was calling me at that time, but I was out of my words, so I changed the topic and cut the call. My body was shivering at that time; I feared that she might tell my brother about that incident. I called her back.

"Hey can you do me a favor. Please don't let my brother know about all this" – I suggested her.

"I didn't have my answer, how did my cell number come to your contact list? Any purpose of calling me?" – she asked.

"No, I just tried to make sure whose number was this, that's it nothing else"- I tried to console her

Girls had lot of mind within them, they know all the tricks how to handle the boys and she was continuously trying to compel me to tell her the truth.

"You have got a melodious voice, that's why I transferred your number to mine without the permission of my brother"- I said frankly

"Did you really saved my number to your phone, judging my voice, I had never been praised for my voice" – she said

"People had lost the judging power within them, so how could they judge your voice, it's really amazing" – I told her

"Someone is calling me talk to you little later"- she said and cut the call.

Chapter 3

Connecting hearts

One day while I was having my studies, a blank message popped onto my screen, an unknown number was there, I continued with my studies. Again after some time a message popped

"Hi, how are you"

"I'm fine but I didn't recognized you"- I said

"I'm the one whose voice you liked earlier"- she said

A patch of current ran through my body. I was trembling, nervousness had overtaken my body. I called her

"Why did you texted me"? A silly question from my side. I banged my head for that.

"Do you have any problem; I will not text you from now"- she added

"No, I am nervous that's why I am saying all these"- I tried to make her comfortable.

She got from my attitude that I was keen interested in talking to her. We both were silent and the call was making money for their operators. Neither I had seen her nor she had, still there was something positive for her inside me.

"Can we be friends?"- I asked her

"Till now what are we?"- A silent shot was given to me

Now the thing was clear, she also had started showing some kind of interest in talking to me. Things got started from here only, we had long hours of continuous call logs, and unlimited calling plans were installed in our cell phones. We had started emerging ourselves into each other. We enjoyed each other's company. We shared our good times as well as bad times together. Nothing meant to us just I & she was there in the scene.

She was a medical aspirant, trying to get a renowned college for her further proceedings. She was intelligent in her studies, she loved to dance, loves to participate in different activities apart from her stories. We matched. Actually I matched myself with every girl in any aspect but this time it was different from others. I hadn't seen her but I was enjoying her company. If I was right she was also enjoying my company.

We never demanded anything from each other; we were just enjoying the filler elements in our empty lives. She completed me and I completed her. It was so simple to handle the conditions between us, the reason behind our emerging friendship was that we were happy in what we had got, we never asked for anything else apart from each other's happiness. We were so close that we shared all the moments regarding our daily schedule. We talked for hours continuously without getting bored from each other.

One day while we were discussing over some topic, suddenly, I proposed her,

"I love you, I have started liking you. I was not able to play with my words as I used to do earlier from other girls, she was different from others"- my heart lampooned.

"Don't embarrass our friendship; I don't want to lose a friend like you" – she urged and cut the call

I tried calling her back but her cell was switched off, she was pissed with my behavior and might switch her cell off because of me. Something was different with that girl; she gave sparks to my body with her actions. She was like a precious stone, which can't be handled so easily. I started having Goosebumps on her name.

"I'm much more when I'm with you"- my heart whispered inside me

While I was preparing myself for my school, I got a text from her.

"I cut the call and you comforted yourself with my no, hats off dear"

I texted her back-

"Immature people always want to win an argument even at the cost of any relationship but mature people understands that it's better to stop that argument so that he can win a relationship".

She was really different from the other girls. She was pure heart and a true friend. I stopped texting her so that she might handle out the condition and forget me because I was not that type of guy who believed in love and all.

But I had started liking her care for me, her prospective to treat me, how she kept me happy. I didn't know what was happening with me, I was losing control over myself.

"My head had got wonderful. Because your picture is inside it"- I texted her

I can't stop myself texting her.

After I came from my school, I saw a number of missed calls and messages were waiting for me, I was tensed what had happened why she called me, texted me. A number of queries were going through my mind. I wasn't stable. I hardly tried to gain control over myself but I failed, it was all her, leaving her imprint on my soul.

"If you had really loved me or cared for me, then you would never have left me like this"- she texted me.

I was feeling sorry for myself, how could I do this to her. I was ashamed of myself. I slapped myself and promised her

"Whatever the condition may be, I am not going to leave your side. I will always be standing beside you."

She was calling and I hadn't the dare inside me to pick her call. Somehow I managed and picked her call

I love you. I really love you- she said & started falling her tears

This was the first time she had been crying in front of me. I was in a situation which demanded love, care, support, but I was failing in all aspects. Till that time love meant me just a word to handle girls, but when she cried in front of me my mindset was changed, I had feelings for her inside me. It was feeling bad when she was crying. It was paining like hell.

I called her

"Now I have confessed what you wanted, if you want this friendship in form of relationship I'm ready for it"- she said

I was shaken by her words she really wanted this friendship to go on at any cost

"Relationships hurts but friendship heals"- she said

She never wanted us to be in such a complicated situation, she just wanted us to be happy. I also decided that I would never let her feel low at any condition, keep her happy and smiling always. We were again back on the same track, as we were earlier lots of chit chats, long duration talks, but she had changed my way of thinking towards any girl.

"Girl's always had the veto power; they can do anything without asking and explaining anyone".

"You wanted me to love you? It happened. Don't know how, when, but I do love you"- she said

"Don't you love me anymore"- she asked terrified

"I really do love you but I didn't know this would come in this way"- I replied

Chapter 4

Immatureness at its peak

I was sitting idle and was thinking about VINNI, my phone beeped, one of my best friends called me and he was sounding pretty low, I asked him the reason but he didn't told me, he asked me to come outside my house as he was on the way towards my home. After half an hour he came, we sat in a park behind my house. He was down with his face and his body language.

"What are you up to? Why don't you come to school? What's going in your mind?"- I asked?

Aashu was a dark, tall, simple guy and he was my best friend during school time. We always used to hang out together, we always stayed with each other. We had a good company. That was the main reason for me to worry about him. He was a good friend of mine.

"I need someone who could understand me and respect my feelings. I need someone to share my talks"- he said

I understood, he needed a girl to hang around. I laughed hardly inside me, what sort of guy he was, upset because he was not able to talk to a girl hahaha.

"You scared me man, I thought something drastic had happened"- I said

"You still think I'm joking or fooling you, please help me with this" – he urged

"Will you be comfortable making friends from my zone"? I asked

"How could I share your friends? It's not the right option"- he added

I must have ended that topic on a NO, but I was keen interested in making one of my friends happy and positive in his life. I forced him and provided her with VINNI's cell number and said

"She is one of the best girls I have met till date and she loves to make new friends, I will give her a call and provide her with your cell number, but please don't disappoint me, she is very good from inside and I can't see her cry".

My mind and my heart were fighting vigorously at that time. I didn't know whether I was wrong or right but I was making someone smile and that had been taught by my parents. He left. I called her.

"Hi, what are you up to. I need to talk to you"- I said

"I'm always free for you dear, tell me what happened"- she said politely.

"Aashu came today at my home and he was very upset and low, he wanted to make a friend whom he could share his views. I tried to console him but he was very down, my mind was not working at that time so I asked him to talk to you"- I said

"I'm not a mood refresher Vicky. How could you do this without asking me, I can't talk to anyone? Will you be happy when I will talk to any other guy?"- She said

"Yes of course, I trust you and that guy too. You are my girlfriend and he is just a good friend of mine who is feeling lonely at this part of his life and needs a friend who could pull him out of his dark life. That's it"- I consoled her

She was convinced by my words and said she would talk to that guy, I exchanged their number

We three were quite happy, our friendship had started picking up its speed. We had group chats on FB and through messages. Aashu knew she was my girlfriend, so there was no problem in our friendship triangle. Everything was going in a perfect manner. We all were happy.

Vinni told me about Aashu that he was good with his heart and he makes her laugh the whole day. She was enjoying his company, and I don't had any problem regarding that matter. Time was passing frequently, she daily talked to Aashu and carry over there talks to me. I was little bit possessive about her.

The next day was my birthday. Vinni was the first to call me

"Happy birthday to you" – a sweet voice was coming out from the other end

I wanted her to be the first to wish me & she didn't disappoint me. My mom & dad arrived at my place for my birthday. As usual I went for my school. I reached my school and found Aashu absent people wished me for my day, somehow I passed my classes, I was eagerly waiting to go home as my mom and dad must be waiting for his me. As soon as the final bell came I rushed towards my home, I entered my room and I was shocked after seeing the scene there, my mom, dad, Aashu and few more friends were busy in decorating my room for my birthday celebrations. I was not aware of any party planning being done by them. I was a happy man from inside, my mom had brought a new dress for me and she had asked me to wear, as we had to go to the temple. I did so we went for the temple and returned before the sun settled. My room was decorated and people were waiting for me to cut my 17'Th birthday cake. My mom knew that I loved to celebrate my birthday that was the reason she arranged these all for me. I loved her. So did she. We partied hard that evening. Food, soft drinks, music all was there to take us to the height of fun. That was a memorable day for me.

Vinni had called me a number of times after she wished me but I was unable to take her call. She messaged me.

"I have thousands of people to entertain me but this heart still needs you".

I loved her and her way of care for me. She had taken my heart

Vinni always asked me to have my studies but I was busy in all other stuffs apart from studies. I had indulged myself with different works and activities, which was not in my favor of my upcoming exams and so was the result, I was expecting supplementary and I got it. The institution fired me and hundred and twenty more students in the middle of a silent road. I was out of my mind, I was not able to think what to do next.

I was in disbelief, suddenly, Vinni called and asked me about my results, I told her that I will talk to her later. My mind boycotted the result on the notice board. What to do next, how will my father react to the situation, a series of questions were popping in my mind and I had no answers of any of my questions.

I blindly blamed Vinni for all these happenings without any reason; I was out of my mind that day. She tried to console me, she called me a number of times but I didn't pick up. She tried to make me comfortable in every sector but I had that wrong perception fitted in my mind that, these all had happened due to Vinni. She was in a deep shock, what had happened to her happy life?

I stopped talking to her, she called me a number of times but I didn't respond, I cut her calls, ignored her messages. I had a mindset in my mind, due to Vinni I indulged myself with other stuffs apart from studies. I added her number to my blacklist

Aashu called me I didn't pick up because he had cleared all his papers and I was little bit embarrassed in talking to him. He had called me a number of times but I was irritated after seeing his missed calls.

An unknown number was blinking on my cell screen, in dilemma, I picked the call.

"Hello Vicky, I need to talk to you" - a known voice was there but I didn't recognized it.

"I didn't recognize you, may I know your name please" – I asked politely

"This is Aashu, where are you man, I'm trying to reach you from quite a long time. I need to talk to you"- he said desperately

"I don't need to talk to anyone, please leave me alone. I need to settle down with time, please don't interrupt"- I requested him.

"I am not interrupting you in your life but just want to say, why have you stopped talking to Vinni? What's her mistake with your result? She has been continuously crying for last night. Why are you punishing her? Please talk to her"- he said angrily

Some other guy was arguing with me for my girl. He was teaching me how to take care of Vinni. He was showing me that she cried the whole night because of me. Screw you man. My anger raised its voice in my mind.

"I don't want to talk on this issue, please forgive me and take care of her, you seem too caring"- I said and hanged on.

I left that town and settled myself in my hometown, it felt like a jail where two wardens were always inspecting me for my work. I had almost lost my all contacts from Vinni, she tried to reach me a number of times but I didn't talked to her. I had indulged myself with my studies and making my parent's dream come true.

One day while I was having my studies in my room, my mom came to me without saying a single word she sat beside me and watching me having my studies, suddenly, she said

"Don't you talk to her anymore? Anything happened between you two? Do I need to know?" - She said sweetly

I was in a state of shock my mom had asked me about Vinni so lightly.

"No mom nothing had happened between us, just a break during the exams my blood- I said.

"I got supplementary in my exams for the first time in my life, I got nervous mom I indulged myself with other activities and made you all feel down. I can't get this pressure off from me until and unless I get something in my life and be a reason of pride for you all"- I said

"Your study is at your place and your friendship is at other place, I know you have skills inside you and you will manage everything positively but you can't blame your friend for the loss of your result"- she said and left.

"It's your mistake Vicky; you can't accuse her on fake issues"- my heart clamored.

When it felt me like that was my mistake I called her

"Hello, I'm sorry"- I said

"No its ok people like me must be treated like this, I deserve this"- she said and started crying.

"Please try to understand my situation I was very down at that time, I had never seen my parents low because of me, I was broken, please forgive me"- I requested her

"No, Vicky you are right at your place, I'm a breaker in your path, leave me and move ahead towards your goal."- She said

"All the best and I'm sorry for what had happened because of me"- she said and hanged on

I was feeling so ashamed of me that I don't even said her bye, at that time my veins were circulating blood but there was no life to live for she had left me due to my silly conceptions. I was missing her in my life but I don't had dare inside me to call her back.

She texted "I know you love me, I understand you more than anyone in this world, I worship you".

I felt that time, I can't let her go. She is the only one for me. I called her and settled our lovable issues together

Chapter 5

First meet

I was at my tuitions, my phone beeped, Vinni had texted me

"Wanted to see you badly, it's been almost six months of our relationship and we haven't spent even a single hour sitting together".

I was also thinking about this meeting from a quite long time but there was no other alternative for me.

When I reached my place I came to know that my father had got a family vacation trip from his company to Goa, as soon as I heard that word of vacation from my father, my mind started making plans.

My father asked me "whether I want to go or not".

"No papa, my exams are there that's why I can't enjoy with you all, you both enjoy the trip- I said

I was a happy man from inside but I didn't showed them, I was sitting in front of them making a sad face as I was very sad, not able to come with them. My eyes were sparkling like a diamond as I had got what I aimed. My parents were going on 25 November and I had also made my plans. My father asked me to go to my uncle's place but my mind had planned something different and exciting.

They were ready with their bags and I dropped them to the station and greeted them a good bye with a saddened face.

I enquired about my train too, and went towards my home for my packing, actually I had not to get anything packed this was just the emerging feelings from my body which had possessed me to think beyond my capacity.

I had three hours left for my train and I was having different imaginations for this awaited trip.

I called my best friend who lived at Ranchi.

"Hello, I am coming to your city get ready for the adventure"- I said in excitement and cut the call.

No reservation, no money in my pocket, my first long distance journey alone and lots of cold but apart from these worst conditions there was an excitement murmuring inside my body to meet my future. I took a general ticket and some bucks from my friends who were supporting me with my journey and headed towards my train. I boarded my train switched my cell to airplane mode so that no one could contact me, I had earlier informed my parents that I was staying at one of my friend's home as he had invited me for his birthday party, so there was no fear in switching my cell off.

I was so excited about that journey that I forgot to wear some woolen clothes, I was wearing a shirt and a hood which was fighting with the cold of Ranchi.

Ranchi had a pleasant weather but in the morning it felt like I was just about to freeze. Cold had arrived there, but I was in love and I was not able to feel it from my heart just the upper portions could feel it.

She was not aware of my plans, she didn't knew I was in

Ranchi, I called her at 6'o clock in the morning.

"Hello, good morning dear"- I said

Perhaps she was in a sleeping mode and just said a yawning "hi".

"I'm here to see you, we both wanted this, and I'm here"- I

Said

Her all sleeping mode had been robbed by my words she was shocked.

"Where are you? Please don't joke my heart is pounding very fast"- she urged

I'm in your town baby, common dress up fast and meet me outside your street I will be waiting for you. At that time I was about to reach Ranchi and I informed her earlier because I knew girls need ample of time to dress them up.

Rahul was waiting for me outside the station, I reached there he handed me with the woolen clothes which I demanded. We went to Rahul's place, I got myself dressed up to meet her and in half an hour we were standing outside vinni's street waiting for her to come.

She was there after half an hour dressed up like a cute Barbie doll, she was looking gorgeous we had met the first time in our relationship. When we met she had tears in her eyes, we were not able to say hello to each other, actually we both had tears in our eyes, and we shook hands and left for Rahul's place.

She was continuously weeping, her eyes were red, and I consoled her that everything is fine I'm here to see you only, I had taken this much of risk for you only, and finally she smiled and hugged me tightly and said

"Don't you ever dare to leave me I will kill you"

"I smiled and said I can't leave you; I will be yours till my last breath."

When I used to be at home, time was like a statue it clicked very slowly but when I was spending my best moments time was running like it had to win a marathon race.

I asked Vinni "Let's go out somewhere"

"No, please I don't want to go anywhere, can't we just seat and talk here only"- she said innocently

"Ok we are not going anywhere. Happy!"- I said

I asked Rahul to get something to eat; we were talking on different topics related to our future and our past.

She was sorry for what had happened due to her, I consoled her that it was not her mistake, I was mentally disturbed at that time and in that condition I accused you that's it, I'm sorry.

First time in my life I was sort of time, it was 3'o clock and my train was at sharp 4.30pm. I asked Vinni

"I had to leave as my train would depart at its scheduled time".

She was down and said- "can't we talk more".

Her each and every activity was taking my heart to her side, her tears were rolling down from her cheeks. I wiped them, kissed her forehead and said we are made for each other and no power in this world could apart us. I love you. I controlled my emotions and greeted her bye.

When I went to drop her, her tears were continuously coming out from her eyes I controlled my emotion and greeted her good bye.

I was at the railway station waiting for my train to arrive, Rahul was there to drop me at the station. I was sad because I don't want to leave that place, tears were falling down my cheeks I wanted to cry but I was hesitating because Rahul was standing with me I tried a lot not to cry, but still I was not able to control my tears, he consoled me not to cry as every moment has its own importance.

I had a feeling inside me, why I came to meet her? My train was about to leave, I greeted him a sad bye.

I had got no reservation I was sitting in the general department, cold was at its peak, I was missing her and the moments spent with her.

I had got a connecting train to my house and I was not about to sleep the whole night as that connecting train was in the middle of the night but when my eyes went down I was not aware of that, my eyes got open when my train had arrived at my destination point and when I got off the train I saw my connecting train was leaving. I rushed towards the train and somehow caught the train. All the gates of the train were closed as I knocked the door of my compartment, one of the cops sitting inside came abusing and opened the door. I tried to console them but they were over me,

They told me that I will be fined under many different sections which I wasn't aware of, I joined my hands and apologies in front of them, they understood my condition and asked me not to repeat these things again. I reached my place but I was feeling like I had left something in Ranchi, "oh my heart was left there because she had kept it with herself".

Chapter 6

Exams planning

It was February and I was preparing myself for the exams. One day while studying, I received a message from Aashu.

"I'm going to meet her"

As soon as I read that text, possessiveness was all around my body. My mind stopped working I didn't have words with me I was thinking of vinni how she could lie to me that she was in no contact with that guy. She knew what I wanted from her. I always used to tell her,

"Whatever you're planning, please let me know, I hate lies

You commit anything wrong let me know, I will sort out the issues but when anyone narrates your mistake, it makes me lose my mental condition".

She knew that I hate lies but still she hide that big thing with me.

Vinni was planning to be a part of her. Aashu wanted her completely.

"My phone beeped".

It was her but I was out of my mind, I didn't want to talk to her, I was shattered by her hide and seek game. After many calls I picked up her call.

"Hi Love"-she said happily.

"Hi"- I replied in anger.

"What's the plan for the upcoming weekends?"- I asked

"Nothing my classes had arranged a surprise test of six hours i.e. two shift papers first shift is from nine in the morning and the second shift is from two in the afternoon. This weekend's schedule is very hectic" –she replied.

"Okay Good. I'll call you later" - I hanged out without any greetings.

"Sunday was two days away". I called it a "Destruction Day."

My mind was blank, I was blank, and how she could lie to me. I knew her but something was there in her mind

I planned that I won't disturb her until and unless she calls me. I woke up late that day when I checked my cell phone, no messages, no calls were there. I was not able to digest that because daily before going for her classes she calls me.

I slept for the whole day and I was irritated as she hadn't called me. She called me at 7'o clock in the evening.

"Hi Love"- a happy hello from her side

"How was your surprise test"- I asked her in a taunting tone.

"It was good paper was so easy but lengthy" – she replied.

I was losing my mind, my face turned red but I controlled myself.

"She was wearing a blue t-shirt and jeans on that day" – My Sherlock Holmes told me.

"You were looking fabulous today in that blue t-shirt" – she was shocked.

"How you come to know what I was wearing, I haven't told you"- she asked surprisingly.

"It's Love" - I said.

"How could you lie to me, don't I Love You"? – I said her

"I didn't lie to you I didn't want to hurt you"- she said

"How was the movie"? - I asked.

"She was silent and a sorry was about to come, but I interrupted between her thoughts please don't be sorry, it was planned, not a mistake".

"I loved you, I saw the world inside you and you lied to me"-I said and cut the call.

Continuous messages and calls were blinking on my cell. I blocked her and dropped my phone to switch off mode. I was crying as I was brooked up with her act. I was burning all her photos. Suddenly, my mom came in and watched me doing that, she was shocked.

"What happened to you? Why are you burning these pictures?" –she inquired.

"Whole world is fake mom, you can't trust anyone"? - I said

I hugged her and started crying.

She consoled me "everything will be ok please have patience and give some time to your friend".

"I am not going to talk to her anymore. I hate people who lie to me, she always lie to me"- I said

"Ok, you have to be honest about your goals which will set up your career, please concentrate on your studies"- she said and on left my room.

"She is my goal mom" I wanted to say that line to my mom but I can't. I wiped my tears and tried to get myself back on track.

At approximately 9'o clock in the night my mom came to my room and handed her cell to me and asked me to talk to Vinni, as Vinni had called on her cell.

"Hello"- I said

It was Vinni, she was weeping, she knew that if she cried I would forgive all her mistakes & that was my weak point.

"Please don't hang up, I need to talk, it's really important"- she said.

"Nothing is there to clear between us, you have to be clear about yourself, what you want from me? I'm not a fool, I have feelings inside me too. You go to that guy I will take you to him but you have to be specific about your mindset without any confusion or hesitation. I will never scold you after that I will be with you forever as a friend but please clear your mind. How could you lie to me? Have I ever stopped you to talk to anyone or to meet anyone?" - I said

"No, I'm not telling that you have stopped me with any of my work but you need to understand my condition, I hide things from you because I don't want to lose you. I always had this fear inside me, that you will leave me, but trust me I love you only"- she said and started crying

"Then why this kind of hide and seek with me, don't you trust me. You know everything attached to me, you know I hate lies. I want to know from your side whatever you had done. Talk to me once and I will forgive all your mistakes. I guarantee"- I said

She was speechless, her voice was breaking badly, and she was weeping for the whole time and she was feeling sorry for what she had did to me in the past.

I knew Vinni, she was an innocent girl but she had to be mature about our relationship, she had to be clear about our relation.

No matter what girls does they had the power to end every discussion with their tears. Actually people like us are emotional fools.

Vinni was different from others, she was a girl who had a golden heart and I knew she loved me a lot but she had some sort of attachment with that guy too. That was the final thought which disturbed me all the time, but I was helpless. I didn't want to restrict her but my heart always did.

After few days we were quite normal as we used to be earlier. I threw that possessiveness out of my body. I made her fly alone in the air. No restrictions, no questions.

I thought that "if she loves me she will stay with me otherwise I don't want a forced relationship". I didn't want her to get hurt, I had opened all the ways for her, and I just wanted to check the power and devotion of my love on her.

"Love needs no boundation it must be left with wings".

My exams were alarming the bell over my head as some emergency had occurred, it was an emergency but we were not aware of it. Few days were left and apart from stretching my mind for the examination papers, I was busy in making plans to meet her and get all sort of problems cleared. Competitive exams forms were out, I filled all the forms and in the entire exam forms one thing was common my examination center which was Ranchi. This time she was aware of the fact that I was coming to her city for my exams.

This was the age where paths were divided, we had to select what kind of path we had to choose. I belonged to a middle class family and we middle class people had the tendency to fulfill all our demands. We care for our fun, we care for our future and all the other stuffs related to our career.

That was me at that time I wanted to keep myself happy, my parents happy but I was distracted from my path, that time I didn't blamed anyone because I knew that was my mistake.

My parents were standing with me at the station waiting for my train to arrive, my body was shaking in excitement, not for the papers but I was going to meet her after a half year almost.

Long distance relationship had different issues regarding different topics but we were quite mature in handling these situations, she never forced me to come and meet her, she always used to say concentrate on your studies which will make your career. I'm always with you whether it's your good time or it's your bad time. She was a girl having lots of sense and intelligence.

I boarded the train and moved to build up my career, a career which was far away from the thinking of my parents. I was not weak in my studies, I had deviated my mind apart from my studies and indulged myself with different works. I was good at my studies till my primary and secondary education but as soon as I was moved towards my further studies, I was degraded. All the links between me and my studies were separated. Study and I were both on different tracks.

We were eight friends on the train no one could see us and tell that we were the examinee of the IIT (Indian Institute Of Technology) paper. We were enjoying our journey at the utmost. We didn't slept a single minute in our journey, very next morning we reached the place for our exams and the whole time table was set by me in my mind how to prepare or execute my papers.

Actually I had prepared myself to meet Vinni and planned a complete two days' vacation plan.

She came to meet me we had the same excitement inside us as we were meeting for the first time.

We met in the day time at the same place where we met first at Rahul's home. She was wearing a white dress and she was looking like an angel, she had taken my heart away from me, she hugged me tightly and she was shivering heavily,

I asked her-"What had happened? Why are you shivering?"

"I'm not responsible for this shivering you have made me like this"- she accused me

"I haven't done anything to you, don't blame me"- I said

"You have made me like this, why the hell you love me this much, that a touch to your body makes my body in a vibrating mode"- she said

"I didn't love you it's your dedication that has blossom the fragrance of love inside me, you have taught me what is love before that I just knew how to play on the name of love but when you came to my life, my mentality got changed I started thinking in a different way."- I said

When I heard you the 1st time on cell, a feeling was there inside me.

"I was lost in my dreams. I was in control but I can't control myself".

"Don't know what was there with that unknown face, I tried stopping myself but still I became hers".

"Distance doesn't matters if your engine pounds for the same body always".

We were in a restaurant behind her house, she was silent, her eyes were down she was not speaking a single word, I was seeing her continuously suddenly she said

"Has anything changed between us?"

"No nothing has changed between us, we are the same as we were at the first meeting do you think anything had changed"- I asked her

We had our lunch together but we were out of words we were sitting quietly and both of us were concentrating on other things apart from each other. God knows what had happened to her this time she was changed and I caught her

"What had happened to you? Why do you seem so low?" - I asked

"Nothing, I'm fine"- she said

We finished our meal and she asked me to drop her home as she was not feeling well. Weather was also changing as she had changed. She was hiding things from me again I can read everything through her expressions. She was so innocent that she can't hide her feelings, by any means she used to tell me what she was up to.

I dropped her home and she promised me to meet me after my exams, we had 2 days of vacation before the exam so we were quite relaxed, we had planned for each and every minute. Me and my friends hired bikes and we were on a tour to investigate Ranchi.

We went to different places and enjoyed the essence of each place.

I and Vinni had planned to visit a famous temple in Ranchi called as 'Pahari mandir'. It was the most famous place as per tourism aspect, people from all over India visit that place. It was lord Shiva's temple positioned on a hill west of Ranchi. The temple was situated on a height of about 2140 feet and people needs to climb approximately 500 steps to reach the summit.

I was having no problem with that kind of height trekking but I was feared of Vinni, she might not get there, I asked her about that but she was more enthusiastic then me, she told me that she had visited that temple a number of times and she would not face any problems. We were passing the stairs very well, suddenly, Vinni asked me that she was not feeling well, I thought she had been tired, I asked her to seat and had rest for some time; I went to bring a water bottle as the summer was on its top acceleration. As soon as I came I saw people had gathered her from all around, I was not able to understand what was going on at that time I was out of my mind. I rushed towards her and saw that she had fainted and people were trying to wake her up but she wasn't,

"She had sinus problem, she is not able to breathe properly at high altitudes"- I said to the crowd

As I said this 'word high altitude' my mind clicked that the place where I had brought her was at the highest altitude in Ranchi. I was shocked what to do then, I tried to wake her but I failed. I sprinkled water droplets on her face with full power, after two or three attempts she showed some sign of positiveness. She had taken my heart away with her.

I thanked people around me and asked them to leave as she was ok.

"Let's go back and I will drop you home- I said

"No, we will go to the temple first and then I will go"- she said

Why girls always keeps on arguing on every topic, nobody could understand them.

"Please try to understand, I can't risk your life and go to that height, please don't make it tough, we will come here again afterwards. Please let's go"- I tried to console her

"No, I had planned to visit here when we were about to meet, please don't stop me I want go to there with you, when you are with me, I don't care what will happen to me, you are there to take care of me, I feel relaxed when I'm with you"- she said politely

I was unable to stop her but I kept a promise from her side that after that she will go to her house. I didn't want her health to be hampered as she was also preparing for her competitive papers. We were at the topmost point of Ranchi, it was the temple full of energy with it. We revered there and we wished for each other and we came down.

I dropped her home and went to my friend's room as they were waiting for me, they had also made some plans to wander in Ranchi and pass their time.

I was tired and was having rest my phone rang at approx. 1'o clock in the night, it was Vinni, and I picked up the call

"Hi baby, how are you"- she asked

"I had not fainted there, so tell me how's you, is everything ok"- I asked

"I fainted because I hadn't ate anything from the last two days, I'm not weak"- she justified

"Good, may I know the reason behind not eating anything from two days?" - I asked

"Let it be, I want to see you now please come and meet me"- she said

"Are you out of your mind, its 1 in the night and you want me to meet you in your house at this time, it's not possible, I'm sorry"- I said

"If you love me then you will be here in half an hour, I will be waiting for you in my garden"- she said and hanged on

I was in a great dilemma, new city, new people, 1'o clock, girl's house ahhh! My mind was working like a supercomputer at that time processing different queries at a single stint. Finally, I decided to roll myself to her house whatever will happen I would see afterwards.

I called her and asked her to be in the garden as I was coming to see her, how could a girl can call a boy to his own house to meet her?

"She adore you stupid"- my heart raised its voice

"Whenever I try to put on pressure on my mind, my heart replies first".

I took my friend's bike and rolled myself towards her house, I was new to that place and I had not remembered the path to reach her house. Somehow I managed to reach her place, there was an army camp situated beside her house and the spotlight which they used to rotate was on but that light was fixed at one place, Vinni was standing there in her garden and she was continuously seeing me and my activities.

I parked my bike far away from her house so that nobody could clasp us. There were barriers on the circumference of her garden but it didn't came into my eye contact as soon as I jumped barriers pinched into my leg but I was not aware of that wound I was targeting to meet her as soon as possible.

She was standing there like a little baby who wants to meet her mom desperately. As I reached there she hugged me, this time the hug was different it had something inside it,

"What happened to you? Why you want to see me this late night"? - I asked

"I wanted to see you that's it no matter what time it is, can't I deserve this much favor from you"- she said

She clamp my hands and asked me to follow her, she was taking me inside her house; I was not able to think what to do at that condition. She asked me to watch for my footsteps as it don't make a noise, I was walking safely somehow a mug was being hit by my leg and it made a crackling noise. Vinni rushed towards her room holding my hands. We sat on her bed, my heart was pounding very heavily, and my mind had stopped working. I did not fear for myself I feared for Vinni, if someone caught us it will be a mess for her, her room was like a prison full of darkness we were talking so silently that only we were able to hear that, she was too happy as I was there to see her.

While we were talking, she kissed me I was shocked as it was the first time for me,

"I love you a lot, my mind always keeps thinking of you"- she said.

I was in a deep thought about girls no one could ever understand a girl's mind. Her elder sister was sleeping beside her and she was normal

"Are you out of your mind? Your elder sister is sleeping on the next bed and you have conveyed me to your room"- I murmured inside her ears

"Nothing will happen no one enters my room without my consent and my Di keeps on sleeping for the complete night and she will woke in the morning itself"- she said calmly

She griped my hands and asked me

"Vicky, I had done so much bad to you but still you didn't change for me. Do you still love me the same as earlier?" - She asked

"I kissed her forehead, do you feel any decrement in my love"- I said

Her face sparkled like a child had got his toy. Unexpectedly, a loud voice came out from outside

"Vinni, is anyone in there with you"- unknown voice

"No uncle no one is here I'm having my studies, cat had made the mug fell from the top that's why the noise was there"- she said calmly

When I came to know that it was his uncle I was like half dead, I tried to hide myself under her tables, curtains. She hold me and hugged me and said nothing will happen to you.

"I'm not worrying about myself, I don't want that anyone point a finger at you. That's it" – I said

"Nothing will happen to me, I know my parents"- she said

I was not capable to breathe properly and I was just pleading to God that no one see us together, somehow I eloped myself from her house and reached my friend's place. We were sitting together from the past two hours, whenever

I was with her time always keeps on accelerating its speed. The very morning when my friends were up I narrated them the uncut story, they were stunned for my act.

Rahul came to me and said

"Are you out of your mind if that spotlight had caught you then there must be a tragical drama with you".

I was just laughing seeing their dramatic faces, I was safe and I was too happy as I had cleared my exam papers quite well.

On the same day my paper was there and I had not slept even for a second. My eyes were red and I was not in condition to go for my papers.

Somehow I managed to dress myself for the papers, it was like i had completed my entire syllabus and i was ready to rock in the exam, but reality was very different.

After the paper, I met Vinni and greeted her bye as my reservation was done by my father. This time she didn't cried and I liked the way she waved me a happy bye.

Chapter 7

Pink city

Competitive papers were over I was rejected by all the department of govt. colleges. I was unable to qualify their marking criteria. All the expectation made by my parents was broken and the only way to make them smile was to get admission in a reputed engineering college.

Engineering was not a word it had heaps of respect hidden inside it. In my locality engineers were respected, being an engineer in small town means a lot to the people living there no matter which institution you studied from.

I didn't craved to do engineering I had been always interested in co- curricular events. I wanted to join NDA but my parents didn't indorsed me for that, they never wanted my selection in NDA. I was low before my dad

And I settled to his terms and conditions. I got admission in one of the most reputed colleges of Jaipur. Vinni was tensed about her future she had inquired me to search a good medical college. One day while I was talking to Vinni, I asked her

"How will it be living in the same city for four years?" – I asked her

"My father had asked me to have admission in the colleges of Punjab, I'm sorry I can't come to Jaipur"- she said

"Ok good go to Punjab your best friend also breathes there"- I taunted

"Why you always use to taunt me? Am I so ruthless? I am not my guardian Vicky, my father treats me very badly I can't even argue with him, he will decide in which college I would study, it's not in my hand dear"- she said

"You could induce your guardian that Jaipur is decent for medical studies not Punjab. Try even once"- I said

"I will try, listen I have to go my mom is calling me"- she said

Vinni talked to their parents about having her studies in Jaipur and her parents got ready in one try I don't know how but they were ready, that decision made me the richest man on the earth. I had removed that lengthy distance relationship tag from us now we both were being admitted in colleges of Jaipur.

College life was welcomed by all with lots of excitement and joy. How one can stop thinking about the college life as this film industries bow their seeds by showing bizarre scenes of college life in their movies. We all had the mindset that college must be like that but when reality comes their whole mindset changes.

My relatives were waiting for me at the Jaipur junction to receive me, I introduce you to an epic personality he is my cousin. He had lots of contact within him he was the master of the area he lives. He had completed his b-tech from a renowned college of the city. My brother dropped me to my hostel and I settled myself there my college was just beside my hostel, I was happy about the forthcoming life which I had to cart on my own. I had to be my peculiar guardian.

SKIT is one of the most renowned college of Rajasthan, it was ranked among the paramount private college in Jaipur province.

Place was decent, people were quiet and calm they don't hinder in anyone's matter. When I entered my college very first day I saw dissimilar students were probing their destination point. They were like the color ball of the snooker which had been hit so hard by the cue ball that they were rive into unlike directions for different purposes.

I loved the campus and the surrounding inside the campus was amazing, people were quite friendly and honeyed. Commencement to the pink city journey was taking my mind to different enthusiasm. I adored Jaipur.

Chapter 8

Four bodies with the same soul

Let me familiarize you to the most imperative individuals throughout my b-tech life

Rohit was a guy who gravitate towards classy things. He was tall, smart, handsome and classic, he was the first person I encountered in my hostel we both were of the similar branch and same class was assigned to us. We daily used to spend utmost of our time together, we were loving our company.

Sandy was my roomie, when I first saw him I thought in what way he could come to engineering, he must be a model. He was tall, well-muscled, intelligent guy. When we met first time we were not capable to introduce each other due to the language difficulty. He was an innocent guy.

Niks was a guy with golden heart, he was like a precious stone which cannot be identified by everyone, and he was something very different from others. He was a friend who touched the inner part of the heart, I had a lot of respect for his friendship.

This was my gang who were always ready for any situation. We all loved each other, respect one's feeling and always used to stay together.

Ragging as this word comes into the market, all the fresher started having Goosebumps inside their bodies. But we were unlike from the starting itself, we don't had any problem or hesitation from the word ragging. Actually people had made a mindset about ragging but now a days ragging had been banned in all the institutes. Ragging is not a physical punishment, it's a way by which fresher could open up and share his feelings and mindsets.

All the students in the hostel were talking about the seniors that they had called all the fresher in the night, we four were giggling at them, we never hesitate to interact with the seniors we provide them with esteem they deserve.

One night while we were relaxing ourselves to our bed, I heard a knock on my door. A voice came from outside

"Open the door and come out, let me demonstrate you all how to respect seniors".

I was shocked what had occurred, it was approx. 11'o clock, I asked my lodger to get up and open the gate but he refused as according to him he was exhausted due to the excursion but I knew the truth, he was hesitating with the seniors, he was little low in relating with seniors.

I gathered some strength and opened the door I was shocked by seeing the milieu had been made outside my room, eight to ten seniors were standing upright outside my room, I greeted them and took my place in the queue where all the fresher were making their way to the seniors one by one. Previously few mates had been introduced in front of the seniors but this was our first time, Rohit was standing just alongside and we were not able to control our smile after seeing the actions performed by our mates. One of the senior started abusing one of the fresher, reason, he was not able to perform the task given by them. I and Rohit saw each other with questioning eyes, fear was crawling down from our faces, but when our chance came they turned out to be liberal we just had to introduce ourselves. "Ragging" word remained always a mess for me, but I never felt occurred in introducing myself whether they were seniors or juniors.

We four were too friendly that was the reason we formed our group within small pause of time, we all were enjoying our group at the utmost.

"Friendship mends happiness and abates misery by doubling our joys and dividing our grief".

We were fitted in each other's block favorably without any concern. One day my warden spoke me in a taunting way

"Let's see how lengthy your friendship stays"

I told him "Our friendship is like rubber you will try to break it will enlarge".

Chapter 9

Place changes mindset

"**When I say I love you more, I don't mean I love you more than you love me. I mean I love you more than the bad days ahead of us, I love you more than any fight we will ever have. I love you more than the distance between us. I love you beyond all the obstacles that could try and come between us**".

Vinni was in Jaipur, we shared the same city, hoping to see each other daily but the bitter truth was that her college was about hundred and twenty kilometer faraway from mine. We were down about our further life ahead.

"Thinking of you keeps me awake. Dreaming of you keeps me asleep. Being with you keeps me alive" - she said.

We had shared a life full of ups and down. We always had our get-together at an interval of 6 months or sometimes a year. We had to be pleased what have we got - I tried to console her but she was aghast.

"Why always us"?? Can't we be laidback?

She gazed at me, I was completely blank.

Whenever I used to be blank, she turn out to be worried. She hold my hands & asked me very innocently

"Can we meet twice in a month"?

Obviously yes, why not— I replied

My girl was as happy as she had got the complete world beneath her feet.

No matter what has happened. No matter what have I done? No matter what will I do? You will love me always. Swear it – she said with crawling tears on her soft cheeks.

She was weeping like a new born baby, she put her head on my shoulder& said-- No matter where I went, I always knew my way back to you. I'm sorry. I'm sorry.

I hugged her & tried to get over the situation but she was continuously feeling apologetic for what she had done. Somehow I consoled her & said--"Whatever had happened I don't care. I respect you & you're indeed care for me. **World seem inaudible to me when you stop talking to me.** Whatever I'm today is just because of you and my parents, you all mean world to me".

As I was sitting next to her a message popped onto her screen, my eyes fall on her display it flashed aashu. She sheltered her screen & gazed at me, our eyes met and she knew that i have seen what had happened in a fraction of second. I didn't interrupted her for that matter. Her face was red & awakened. I always used to say her that **"Hurt me with the truth rather than comforting me with a lie".** But this time I was silent looking for her reaction to the situation, so was she like a stand-up statue.

It was a rapid change of mindset of –"Why always us to Why always me??"

I simply greeted her bye and I was on the way to my college.

Long journey came to an end as we reached our place. We were quite exhausted after that hectic journey. That text was hitting my mind continuously, my eyes were red, and not because of that particular text but because of the carelessness we showed at the time of journey. We were in a situation, if a cop catches us we had to pay him a huge amount for violation of guidelines. We had no authentic papers, no license, and no helmets. We had been like the biggest accused person if we had been caught, but thanks to the almighty we were home safe. As soon as I reached my place my cell pooped it was her but I didn't pick.

I was on my couch finding my dreams to hold my hands but when dream found me I didn't knew. I was in my stressed out position trying to get all my concern out of my body. Rapidly, I heard a voice in my ear; it was my own cell ringtone. I woke up, 10 missed calls were waiting for me. It was hers. I called her but she didn't pick up. After half an hour she called back

"I called you a number of times but you were out of this world "- she shouted angrily.

'Half of me was conscious but the other half still was in dreams'. She was shouting heavily at me and I was yelling hmm hmm in response to her.

She was irritated. She was pressing her teeth onto each other; voice of pissing her teeth was coming out clearly my mind got disturbed,

"Why do you think I should always be available for you?"- I asked angrily.

Because you adore me- she said so sweetly that my heart got melted but I didn't show her.

Why aashu texted you?? This time I was solemn

"Nothing..."- Her voice broke up. I got her this time

Having faith on each other is the basic fundamentals of a happy love life- I said her calmly.

"He is only a good friend of mine, there is nothing to worry about us"- she said as nothing had happened in the past & cut the call.

My possessiveness was at its high a single word flashed on the screen and my mindset was completely changed, perhaps this could be due the immatureness I had inside me for her. She treated me like a child. She loved me, I loved her. We were always been there for each other whatever the situation had been we never changed.

I hit the wall so hard that the tremors coming out of the walls said- never hurt yourself for anyone's deed. Situation compel questions to be hard otherwise answer always lie within its range. Complications had become a copyright to our story, wherever we went it followed.

Chapter 10

Birthday present

Classical guy was in his 18. 27ᵗʰ September was his day. In my town birthday was welcomed warmly and gracefully but picture was different here, all the warm welcome to the birthday was given by hands and legs. Once the b'day victim celebrates his day in any of the institution, he would never imagine of celebrating his birthday throughout his life.

Planning were been made for him too, not to arrange the cake and other eatable but how to hit him and wish "Happy Birthday".

"People regret to celebrate their birthdays here"- one of my senior told me before.

I got my answers "why to repentance on birthday"

Engineers called birthday as

B- Bad and D-day.

Mr. Classic was little bit downhearted on his day. He was not feeling healthy since two days and was scheduling to celebrate his day with his family. We were also down especially Sandy was low as he was not able to show Rohit, the power emerging through his body. He was keen interested in hitting Rohit on his birthday but Rohit was not fighting fit so he had to satisfy by a prescribed birthday wish. We had less time left with us as Rohit had to leave for his house, their parents were continuously calling him regarding his health as he was not well.

"We had to cut his cake earliest by nine"- I announced

We all gathered in our gallery to celebrate his birthday, he was not able to open his eyes properly due to the fever. Somehow we cut his cake and sang birthday songs for him. He was in a hurry as he was about to go, we dropped him to the rickshaw stand.

I was sleeping in my room and was thinking of Vinni, I saw an old message in my cell, it was vinni's message

"Call me when you are free"

Busy! Busy! Busy. I was continuously calling Vinni but she was busy with her work at 2'o clock in the morning. My mind again clicked that name and my temperament was not under my control.

"I can stand her even if she doesn't loved me but I can't stand her loving him". -I murmured inside me

Relationship is like thread it goes well until and unless a knot take place in it.

At approximately 3'o clock my phone beeped, it was hers. I picked up in a single ring.

"Have you finished or will take some time to accomplish your mission- I asked

"Why always you take him wrong. He is my best friend- she persuaded me

It always kept me irritated that my girl argues with me for the person I hate the most.

"Your Girl"- My heart lampooned

She was turning out to be hers.

"Girls do have best friend?"- I taunted

Why always girls need a backup? I was cut of my mind.

"You think I'm entertaining both at same time"- she was low that time.

"No I didn't meant that but why you compel situation to be hard"- I asked instantly

"He is not my boy, just a good friend I love to hang out with"- She excused me

"Oh you love hanging out with that guy, then you must have something for him inside you" – I concluded

I'm coming to Jaipur tomorrow to meet you. Let's meet and talk- She said and hanged up.

I messaged her

"You ignore my love on the name of possessiveness but if you had seen the pain inside my heart you must had stopped ignoring it".

His birthday was turning out to be awesome, he was celebrating his birthday and I was handed with different types of gifts by my love. She had been burning me from inside, she was unaware of the fire inside me, and she was adding different burning materials inside my head which was burning my body and my heart slowly.

Once again happy birthday classic guy and thanks for the gifts my love.

Chapter 11

Heart's Clamor

I was standing at Narayan Singh circle waiting for my soul mate, as she was approaching to Jaipur to talk on aashu's issue. Black color suits her and yes she was in black marching towards me, how much anger I had inside me, all melts down when I see her, she was like a therapy for my raised anger. I loved the way she controlled me, she knew my all weak as well as strong points. We had the same soul in two different bodies.

She was upset, she was here to debate such an issue which I loathed the most. Literally, that guy was creating scene in my cheerful life.

We hired an auto rickshaw and went to one of the well known temple in Jaipur ie Birla temple, we were planning from a long time ago to visit that temple finally we went, after we had our rituals we sat on the stairs of the temple. She was observing the world over but she wasn't eyeing at me, don't know why but someone was functioning inside her brain.

"Can we talk? What you wanted to talk?" - I said

No response came from her side, it seem like she was completely disregarding me perhaps, she didn't need to talk to me.

"You must find a better girl Vicky; you don't need to fry your brain due to my deeds"- she said breaking up her silence.

"I think you have your boy with you, that's the reason you are suggesting me to select any other girl, do you think that I would go for any other girl apart from you"- I said in taunting way.

"See Vicky my parents will never be ready for us, my father needs a boy who must be of the same caste. He will never allow me to stay with you" - she clarified

Oh! Now you are aware of these class and religious conviction, you had to tell me in the starting about all these I must have not fallen this much for you. I have told my parents about you" – I said in a taunting way

What I was saying in anger I was not aware of that.

"Shattering of promises was started, why people promise when they know there is no future ahead".

She was leaving me and I was standing there like a statue I was not stopping her because my parents had taught me never call a person from behind when they are leaving. She seemed different that day, she was ignoring me and my talks, and she was forcing me for any other girl. She was not my girl. She was speaking someone else language.

"We are good friends and we will be till my last sniff, we will always stand for each other whatsoever the condition may be"- she said

Love had been converted to decent friends, stage changes people, so was she, her face was showing some essence of betray, she had left my side and she was preparing to stand herself on the other side of the road opposite to me

"Love is called as heaven, when everything goes on the right track but life becomes hell when any of the tracks has been damaged".

I was listening to her shattering talks but I was not able to utter a single word, my body had freeze due to her talks. Each and every word coming out from her mouth was like a bow, which was penetrating deep inside my body. She had no guilt on her face, she was quite normal or she was pretending to be normal I didn't knew that, I was thinking of my further life, she had made me stand in a situation where both side was totally dark.

I was afraid of those talks; I tried to change the topic but she was here with a feeling to make as many holes as she can in my body.

"Can we eat something?" - I asked her

"No I don't want to eat, let's go I get you your favorite burger"- she said

"Why you care for me, when you want me to have an another girl in my life" – I said

"I asked you to go to another girl because I don't deserve you this doesn't mean that I stop caring for you, why should I stop?" – She said confidently

"You have lots of guts inside you, you are arguing with me on the topic which I hate the most and from now I hate you too, you both had made my life worst"- I said in anger.

Finally we moved towards Gaurav tower a place full of life. It was the place which beats in every youngster's heart of Jaipur. From a child to an old age people GT welcomes all; it was the place for everyone.

We always used to come to that place, we were at a dosa shop, and Vinni liked dosa a lot, so we were having dosa in our lunch.

She was not allowing me to eat with my hand she was nurturing me with her hand I stopped her, but she was busy with her work without listening to me. I hated her but this heart always compels me to stand on such a situation where I had to make tough decisions.

We were on the edge of changing our relationship status but she was still showing the same care she used to show me. I knew it wasn't love but still I needed whatever it was, I was showing her that I don't need her but from inside I was dying to get her.

"I was having pain in my heart which could be known by only one who had lost his world before getting it and I was that person".

I felt helpless at that time, I wanted to hug her but my mind stopped me, I wanted her to go away from me my heart stopped me. I was like hanging in the middle of the road, I can see both the side of the road but I wasn't able to take any of them. Girls had this habit they always show dual side of their life which confuses people like us. I was very confused at that situation, my heart was making noise to make her stay but my mind asked me to let her go.

I had stuck myself in a fight between my heart and my mind, both were correct at their own places but I was confused about the choice I had to make.

"I'm getting late for my college, I have to leave"- she said

I was upset as she was leaving Jaipur and me too, she had provided me with the hint that her father will never be ready for me which meant she was saying good bye to our relationship. I told her that I was going to drop her to her college, she agreed and the bus picked its speed.

We had crossed half of the distance, Vinni was sleeping she had kept her head on my shoulder, I was seeing her face from a long time, she seem so cute and innocent. After two hours of journey we reached her college, I woke her up and greeted her bye. When she was gone I felt like I had missed something, I hadn't missed something I was losing her. I get myself a bus and returned back to my place.

I reached my room and tried calling her

Busy! Busy! I laughed at my fortune, switched off the cell and slept. I was tired, mentally as well as physically.

Sandy was standing beside my bed like a leaning tower and was watching me from a long time.

"Your mom had been trying to reach you from a long time ago, where is your cell phone?" – He asked

"My phone is with me but its battery is low that's why it's switched off"- I said

Talk to your mom she was willing to talk to you from a long time ago.

I called my mom

"Hi mom, how's you?"- I asked

"I'm fine beta, where were you I was trying to reach you from a long time?"- She said

"Oh one of my friend had come to Jaipur to solve some issue with me"- I said

"Vinni had come and you don't inform me" – she said

My mom was a genius. I loved her.

Chapter 12

Puzzled race

As days were passing lots of work load was imposed on my back by my branch, I was busy with my college agenda and daily I was left with such a small period of time which was not sufficient to bear out vinni's demand. I hardly had time to eat and sleep. She was stressed with my timetable, she daily calls a number of time but I was not able to pick her call and when I receive notification of her call, I was bordered by my dreams. Due to the work load I got tired and as soon as I reach my place only one thing gets in my perceptiveness that was my bed, I hurriedly hug my bed without changing my dress and without having my dinner.

We were not able to connect properly because of the fitted routine of the college. But I always strained to talk to her but, "when fortune is not our side nothing could modify the result". When I called her she kept busy with her work and when she called I was distracted in any of the works. We was moving under the shelter of misunderstandings which looks fine from outside but it works like a termite which destroys stuffs from inside.

Situation had also started making fun of us, life had taken a wrong path and on the top of these were the mobile networks they worked as "ice on the cake". Whenever we talked these signals starts showing its strength, we kept listening to each other's 'hello' and nothing more than that, she felt that I was ignoring her but truth remains truth we can't change that.

I called Vinni. Busy!

"The number you are trying to reach is currently busy" a recorded voice came to my ears. I tried few more times but she was still busy. I was thinking who could it be, suddenly my mind strike a name aashu I was down. Men like him keeps on waiting for the exact time to steal someone's soul.

But i wasn't sure that whom she was gossiping to, so I called aashu to confirm their call match.

As the moon was surrounded by its cloud preventing its brightness to reach us so was that guy preventing my love to reach her.

As the call picked up its way my heart start pumping blood heavily, I wished she might not talking to aashu, but she was talking to him as aashu's cell was also busy.

I abused him inside me and banged my phone down.

I tried continuously but they both were busy in gossiping with each other. At approximately 3'o clock my phone rang it was Vinni, I cut the call and kept the cell in vibrating mode but she was continuously calling me, twenty four missed calls were flashing on my cell phone, she kept calling and I kept ignoring her this drama lasted for fifteen minutes. After that I picked her call and kept my phone alongside.

"What happened? Why you are not picking my call?"- She said exhaust.

"Go and exchange your talks to that bastard & don't you dare to talk to me, I had picked your call say you that don't plea me."- I said in anger

"Please grow up and don't be egoistic all the time, aashu had got tumor inside him. Be generous Vicky!"- She said to me

"Please stop giving me these emotional pleas. I'm afraid of your motives"- I said in anger

"I'm not giving any excuses, that fellow is admitted in the hospital in Chandigarh. Why you do upkeep only about yourself?"- She said

"Oh! Your heart started pounding for your dreamed one. Let's confirm whether he is admitted in hospital or not, let's talk in conference me, you and that guy."- I said

She said no and cut the call. I was shocked by that stroke of her, she was not like that but she was turning out to be, due to the mind games played by aashu. He had been deviating Vinni from me by his silly tumor type talks, I knew she was not guilty and can be fooled and I was right that guy was frolicking with the emotions of Vinni and she was taking that guy right. I decided to call aashu.

"Hello, how's you? I heard that you have tumor inside you"- I said

"No brother I'm quite well, just to keep her on my side I told her that I had tumor inside me. You know it's quite easy to fool girls like her"- he said

"Please don't you dare to call me brother, guys like you eats their own egg and if you tried to deviate her then I will show you how tumors are taken out from the body"- I threaten him

"Oh! I got feared by your forewarnings, go to your girl and request her not to call me or go to a psychiatrist for your lookover you are not capable to see that your lassie is fooling you"- he said

"Thank you for your suggestions you just do one thing discontinue coming in between us else I am going to abolish your whole life"- I said and hanged on

Vinni had been calling me from a long time. Finally, I picked her call

"What are you up to Mr. Vicky?"- She said

"Nothing, I just trained your friend a good class"- I said and hanged on

I switched off my cell and was thinking of Vinni, how she had transformed but I was not getting the reason overdue her change. I never cheated on her the only mistake from my side was that I was not able to deliver her ample of time to talk to me. I thought

"The boy must had something within him as he deserted my ocean of love with his new tides"

Chapter 13

Vacation Time

At that time semester exam was on the topmost priority. Sessional, practical, midterms all were creating their way together to haunt student like us. But we were quite relaxed at that situation, we carried a quote with us **'more study more problem, no study no problem'**. My group indulged themselves with the other activities throughout the whole semester but as soon as exams knock their door, they became vampires. They hunt down the complete syllabus in a night or two.

One of my seniors had told me 'engineering papers were one night fight'. And all the engineers were master at this socket.

I had no strategies for my exam, I was busy in making plans with Vinni. Vacations were convincing students to go to their home, my hostel was empty in a day or two only my group was left to depart. My mind clicked to spend some time with Vinni and I told her about my plans and she agreed. We were the happiest couple at that time, we were about to spend 3 days together, we made diverse plans, how to make that vacation surpassed. We were in love for a second time, this was the first time we were trying to start a new year together.

Mr. Classic was planning to make his way to his home for the vacations and for the preparations of exams. We were at the bus stand waiting for his convenience to arrive. We were quite hungry and searching the suitable place to feed ourselves. Finally we found a famous shop named as 'Santosh dal bati house'. Dal bati was the traditional food in Rajasthan; people love to click their tongue with that special dish, this dish always left me with a feeling of 'litti chokha' of my hometown.

As soon as we finished our meal his bus arrived, we greeted him bye and was about to move to our respective places, suddenly my cell vibrated, it was an unidentified number I picked up

Hi Vicky- a recognized voice was there on the other side

Hello, who is this? I didn't recognized you- I said

This is Robin. Where are you at this time? You have to arise to my place for my b'day fete. We will have the ceremonial dinner together- he said and drooped the call

I told Niks and Sandy about this, Sandy asked me to come with them as that zone was not safe to feel free. I argued with sandy that my friend had called me for the first time and I need to go. By some means I lent a cab and went to the b'day bash. Cab motorist was not at his top, he was stoned and he was driving very coarsely, I asked him to slow down but he was so high that he didn't responded to my question.

"Where the hell have I trapped myself? Please anyone stop this senseless driver"- my mind lampooned.

I was unceasingly saying that driver to drive easily and securely, but no, he had sworn on my name that he will offer me with an audacious voyage. I asked him to slow down but he was continuously increasing the pressure on his right leg. My phone was vibrating from a long time but I was so frightened by that driver that I was not able to pick the call, somehow I collected my power and picked up the call. It was my friend asking me where was I? I wanted to tell him that I had stuck to a drunk drivers cab and was about to lose my life but I didn't told him about all these, I didn't want to spoil his day.

We were just few meters distant away from his dynasty, I was using my cell phone. BANG! my driver had did what I was dreaded of, he had hit his car to a bended tree, I was out of the car and I was not in a condition to get myself in a standing position. While there had been a number of coincidences on that way over the winter month. But at the time of crash, the surface was dry and the temperature was high than its normal point and my cab driver was heavily drunk which increased the chance of accident.

Somehow I managed to pick my cell and called my friend who had invited me for his happy celebrations and I had made his day worst, I called him and said I had met with a major accident outside your street please come soon, with those words my eyes were closed automatically. I was color in red and I was not able to move my body, my eyes got closed automatically.

When I opened my eyes, a panel of doctors were standing in my ward, my head was bandaged, my hand was plastered overall my whole body was wounded with scratches and cuts. It was late night when I opened my eyes, my whole body was grieving like the most dreadful pain anybody had, and I was not able to move a single inch from the position which had been specified to me by the medics. I was in immense pain, I called up my acquaintance and asked him to call the clinician and tell him about the pain emerging through my body. In few minutes one of the attendants was there, he provided my saline with pain killer doses and sleeping doses.

I was worried about the vacations which we had planned for that merry month, all had been ruined by that cab driver. I was pondering 'Change was the law of nature, nothing was permanent. We can't stick ourselves on a single plan; we never know what had been planned for us by the almighty'.

December had arrived, the merry month we was moving our lives in a cheerful way, we both were pretty pleased about the awaited vacations but deity wanted something better than that, she was trying to reach me from a long period but I was unable to interact her. I assembled some power and called her'

"Hi baby, can we meet tomorrow"- I was low while speaking

"What had happened? Is everything ok with you"- she got my low voice

"If you will listen to me calmly without being panic I would tell you something"- I said

"Please stop jumbling the words and tell me what had happened. My heart is pounding at a very high rate"- she said

"I had met with an accident and i am admitted to an orthopedic hospital. Will you be able to meet me tomorrow"- I requested

"I will be there before you will be up baby, you are my strong kid please don't panic and sleep calmly everything will be ok"- she said and hanged on

I knew why she cut the call; she was not able to show her tears in front of me, her voice was shaking when she was consoling me. I called one of her friend and requested her to be with Vinni as she would not be able to handle this situation alone. I was in lot of pain. I called a number of friends and relatives, as I was not able to make myself sleep and I informed all my friends about the incident. When my eyes went off I didn't knew. My parents were informed about the incident and they were on the way to meet me. They were tensed and worried about my health so was I worried about their condition after listening about me.

I woke up very early because of the pain inside my body. I called my mom.

She picked my call in a single ring which showed the desperate nature of a mother towards his child.

"Hi mommy, how's you, when you all are reaching here"- I asked

I asked a series of questions in a heavy voice to show her I am all ok but she was my mom, she knew everything

"Don't show me your heavy voice that you are ok, I know you more than you know yourself" –she said

"I'm fine mom just a few scratches and cuts had been imprinted on my body, rest, I'm all ok I had been surrounded by lots and lots of friend, you need not to panic" - I consoled her and hanged on

It was 7 in the morning, somebody knocked my door, I asked him to come in, a number of known faces had arrived to see my tragic condition. There were approximately 10-15 people in my room. Niks, sandy and many more friends were there, vinni's friend had also came to see me but the face I wanted to see at that particular time was not there, she was standing outside my room as she was not able to see me in that condition. I asked one of her friends to call her inside, actually Vinni was trying to wipe her tears, making herself comfortable and relaxed before meeting me. She entered the room as soon as she saw me she was not able to control her tears she ran away out of the room. Sandy came to me and sat beside my stretcher and said

You never listen to us; you always do work according to your way. I stopped you but you didn't. See how she is broken up after seeing you like this- he said and left the room with tears in his eyes

All the people standing in that room was sad on seeing me I was the only person smiling at my fortune that I had got a number of good friends who had surrounded me during my bad times. I called Vinni and asked her to come inside. She came and sat beside me and said

"I hate you. You are a cheater"- she accused me and started crying.

She holds my hands and kept it on her cheesy cheeks and she was continuously compelling her tears to roll onto hand. I can't see her cry, my weak point.

"Handle yourself carefully. It's not yours. You are the reason of happiness to someone's life"- she said

Suddenly, a panel of doctors and staff came into my room and asked me if I had some pain or not.

"No, sir"- I answered simply

Doctor called up one of my friend and asked him to follow towards his cabin. I was disturbed why the doctor had called my friend to his cabin. After half an hour panel of doctors again entered my room behind them sandy and Niks was standing with their sad faces. Their eyes met mine, I smiled but their faces didn't match their smiles. I was worried what had happened to them, why the doctor had called them. Something was there in their mind which was disturbing them, I called Niks and asked him what had happened, but he didn't told me anything about their talks, sandy came to me and whispered in my ears,

"Head and hand injury has to be operated"

"For god sake, don't let my parents know about the head surgery"- I murmured inside Sandy's ear

My hand was wrecked badly, it had been in three parts, and x-ray reports were telling all the truth. One of the nerves in my brain was pressed onto the other; this was the main reason of concern. 'Head surgery was not a joke'. All the agreement papers were being ready and signed by my roommate on his own risk.

"Whatever will happen our team will not be responsible for any loss"- one of the doctors said

Vinni was unaware of the situation what was going inside the room because doctors had asked them to stand outside the room. Sandy and Niks came to me and asked me to had rest as the doctors were planning to operate me as soon as possible. Both of them were hyper tensed. It was 3'o clock in the afternoon and Vinni had to leave for her college, so I didn't let her know about that issue. I asked her to leave as she will get delayed for her college. She left me with a smile, i asked one of her friend to take care of her as she will panic thinking of me.

As soon as Vinni and their friends left, again all the doctors came to my room but this time they were not here to ask me about my health, they were here before the process of operating me. My friends were watching me in the way that it was our last contact with them.

I smiled at them and said- "I'm never going to leave your side idiots". They burst into laughter and hugged me and wished me luck for my operations.

I was keen busy with my doctors as they were injecting me, dosing me with their pain killing antidotes and getting me ready for further undertakings, which had been signed by my mates. Stretcher was there in my room to take me to the operation theatre, 4-5 attendants were there in my room to hold me up and settle me onto the stretcher, my heart was beating at its high rate, and I asked sandy to stay with me. Two of the attendants hold my hands and two were down at my leg, they hold me and put me on the stretcher. It was disturbing a lot. I controlled my anger and pain my mind murmured 'why the hell they picked me up from that comfortable position'.

Tears were rolling down my face but I was smiling seeing my loved ones, they were always with me at my good times as well as bad times. My stretcher was being trundled towards the operation theatre, now that was my turn to had Goosebumps inside me.

I was shifted to the operation theatre and I was dressed using the patient outfits and I was enclosed with a white blanket and an oxygen mask was put up on my mouth. I was anxious and I was quivering. I asked one of the assistants

"Will it pain while operating. Would I be able to knob the pain"- I asked?

"Nothing will happen you will not be able to feel any of the activities happening in your body"- he said

Lights were on, my friends were circumscribed outside the operation theatre.

As I was lying down on my stretcher a doctor came to me and said 'don't be worried the whole thing is going to be alright just support us, all the best'.

You will feel just a pain of injection and it would be the last pain during the whole operating process. Anesthetics were the best to make a person senseless during the procedure of operation; they injected me on the neck with anesthesia, it was like an electric current which had been entered through my body. I was shuddered by that injection, after that injection they opened the bandage from my head and that plaster from my hand, it didn't hurt that time, I was shocked after what I had saw, anesthetic had started showing its effect. They covered my face with that bed sheet and what happened after that was just felt by me because I was not able to see what was going outside that bed sheet.

I was senseless but I had not collapsed, I could feel what was going on with my body. Scissors, drilling machine and many more operating tools were tested on my body.

After 4 hours of operating process I was out of that room, a room with lots of gravity and pressure, finally doctor gave me a smile and said

'You need not to worry now you are ok'.

I was not able to speak anything because the doctors had stopped me to do so as there was ample of blood loss inside my body. As soon as I was out of that room, I saw my mom standing beside the gate of my room she had tears in her eyes but I ignored her because if I had the eye contact with her I can't stop myself. She was watching his operated child which had got a new birth. She was crying due to the happiness inside her when the doctors told them that I was all ok.

I wanted to talk to my mom, I wanted to say her thank you for coming but I was not able to speak a word because of the oxygen mask. I was smiling at my fortune.

My planning always gets shattered, I had no worry about my health, I was thinking of the vacations which I and Vinni had planned before that accident.

I was kept under surveillance for couple of days, when I was discharged from the hospital, doctor counseled me to have a complete bed rest for 45 days, but this time my holidays came at a very erroneous stage and that was before my semester papers

Chapter 14

Reunion

I was on the train waiting for my station to attain; that was a hectic journey with broken hand and head. I was irritated after that 18 hours journey. At the end of the day I was a happy guy as I was going to meet my parents. I received many messages and call from the relatives, they were keen interested in meeting me as I had won an award in an event. When I steeped on my soil, many of my relatives and friends were present there to see me. They were quite tensed when they saw my state I had bandage on my head, hand was plastered. They greeted me good luck for my sooner recovery.

I reached my place and met my mom over there she was dying to see her child face. She hugged me and welcomed me as if I had arrived after years.

'Mom it's been only 6 months. I'm ok now no need to panic yourself'- I said

"This is a new birth to my child, how should I not welcome you warmly"- she said and started crying

"Oh why always ladies cry on every topic"- I murmured slowly

"Because their heart are not as callous as we have"- he fussed into my ears.

Father is always a son's father, we can't overtake them, and they always stay ahead of us.

He asked me to settle down and he handed me with a glass of juice, I knew that, my recovery process had been started. And my father had appointed himself in the advancement of my well-being. I was very happy after seeing my parents relaxed. When my eyes got closed I didn't knew that.

"Vicky open the door"- someone shouted

I asked my mom to see who was calling me; mom went to see who was there,

'Rahul' had come to see you – she shouted

My born and best friend was there to see me, I was so excited after seeing him that I tried to get up from my bed, but I was failed. I felt like a paralyzed person who can't carry out his work on their own.

He came to my room carrying tears with him, he tried to hide it from me but he failed I caught him.

"I thought men like you had strong feelings regarding these situations, but you made my prediction wrong. You were crying I saw you"- I taunted him

"Don't you teach me the lessons of emotions and situations, if anything had happened to you, I would have broken your jaw? We love you and don't you dare to hurt yourself anymore"- he was serious. He made me sit and sat beside me, he was having the same question on his face which everyone had.

How the accident took place.

I answered his questioned face "I was in a cab and the cab driver was drunk and he did the rest job, I was not responsible for my accident"

"I know you don't lie to me"- he said generously

Rahul was on his vacations. He was having his studies in one of the best engineering colleges in Karnataka.

He was the type of person who keeps on improving his skills in all departments. He was intelligent, aggressive and smart in all his works. He was a type of person whom everyone can call a 'perfect personality'. He was like a brother to me, we were friends since sixth class, and in starting I hated him a lot because he was a type of guy who kept himself involved in all the other activities but later on he kept improving his standards and finally he was on the top of everyone. My parents adore him. He was like my elder brother who guided me at every point in my life. He was like an idol to me.

We had planned a lot for the vacations but all in vain, nothing was on its track time had changed every plan made by me

Rahul cell beeped, it was Priya, and he handed his phone to me

"Where are you Rahul? I'm waiting for you outside Vicky's house please come fast"- she said

"Please let your legs move and come inside"- I said sweetly

"I don't want to talk to you, please give the phone to Rahul"- she said

"I'm coming out to see you stay there"- I said

"No! I'm coming up, please you stay in your bed and have rest"- she said hurriedly

She met my mom and dad but she didn't came to my room. I knew the reason she can't see me like that we were friends since class four, we had shared a lot of memories together, we were best friends. We always used to fight from each other over small things but we cared for each other a lot. She was not able to see me like that, which was the reason she was not coming in my room. I called her but she didn't picked up, after some time footsteps were reaching my ears which meant she was coming to see me her eyes were down she was not able to make eye contacts with me she came beside me and hit me on my thighs and said

"For the world you are just an ordinary person but you mean world to us so don't you dare to hurt yourself anymore"- her voice was breaking but she controlled her feelings she was about to burst into tears but she managed herself.

She loved me like his own brother she used to care for me a lot. I loved her too. My whole body was shivering by her words, she got me and changed the topic

"What about your Miss Priority? How is she?"- She asked

"You all started again don't use your brain on this topic let it be on my side only. When I started loving her, I didn't asked her for the promise that she will also love me the way I love her. Whatever she did to me or whatever she will do, I accept her as my first and last love"- I said her

"Let me ask you one question Di?"- I said

"Have you ever been so broken that you started laughing on your own condition and suddenly burst into tears? My situation could be understood only by one who had lost his world before getting it"

"That's why we always force you to move on don't stick to a girl who is not sure about her future, she is just playing mind games with you"- she said in anger

"I can't leave her I see something in her eyes for me. I don't mind whether its love or her immense care towards me but whatever it is it increases my strength to love her more"- I said politely

"End your important topic guys I have got some eatables for you all"- my mom interrupted

We all had our lunch and we were sitting and gossiping with each other suddenly Priya's phone rang, it was her mom and she was asking Priya that when she was coming to home. The bell had alarmed for her she was about to leave.

How clock runs away when you were out with your best friends spending good moments. Priya had to leave for her home, Rahul dropped her to the bus stand.

It had been always amazing to spend times with your old friends but when they leave it hurts. I was down and I was just about to sleep suddenly my phone beeped. A beautiful name was blinking on my screen but I was not able to pick the call because of my parents sitting beside me, she called a number of times but I was in such a condition in which I was not able to pick the call. She left with a message

"How could you know what is emptiness ask those broken leaves what is being in despair. Don't you dare to accuse me on the name of cheat; Ask this time when I don't remembered you"

We had lost almost all contacts between us. I was bounded with the situation so we were not able to connect each other, whenever she called someone must be around me and due to this circumstance I was not able to pick her call or reply to her messages. This accident had created an essence of separateness between us.

I was also helpless, I was not able to stop my fortune to ruin my happy love life.

One day I was sitting alone in my room and then my mind clicked that this could be the best time to call her

I called her

"Hello"- a sweet voice was fussing into my ears

"Hi baby, how's you? I'm sorry. I was unable to pick your call, I'm also helpless dear, and I have been always surrounded by different people"- I said

"No issue I had learned to live without your voice, I had adjusted myself according to the situation"- she said taunting at me.

But this time her way of talking was different, she was quite normal and she was talking to me without scolding me.

Do you know one thing Vicky?

"When tears fall it had no sound with it when heart shatters it had no sound with it if you had got the pain inside my heart you could have stopped ignoring me"- she said

"I'm helpless Vinni try to understand my condition" – I said

"Don't you have ten minutes for me, it's tough for you to take out ten minutes from your busy life"- she said

"No I don't have any time for you until and unless you understand the complexity of the situation, if you are ready to live with me like this then its ok otherwise you have your choices"- I said in anger

"What you said I have choices, what sort of choices you are talking about Mr Vicky"- she said in the same tone as I did

"Oh you are a single man woman, you only talk to me and you don't know anyone except me. Right?"- I asked

"No I'm not in contact with aashu. Sometimes he texts that's it don't you apply your brain in other issues there is nothing between us"- she justified her words

"How you came to know I was talking about that guy I didn't utter his name?"- I asked

"You didn't talk to me for weeks and if someone texts me at an interval of days then you have problem with that guy. I'm also human Vicky I also need people to share my words. I live in such a place where people used to live separate and I always used to be alone in my room. I need you to support me but you are becoming too possessive at the present situation"- she said

I was being possessive, if I showed some care for my girl then I was desperate for her. Wow! What a remark had been given to me by my girl. I was seeing Vinni on the other side of the road, she was speaking aashu's language.

"I'm what I have to you don't need to judge me"- I said and hanged on.

Chapter 15

Turning 19

"**Why should I always call her to come back, didn't she know nothing is there with me except her**"? - My mind lampooned

"**We had no reason to fight still one wants to be alone, this doesn't mean that we need break from our relationship. We must respect ones decision and give space to other**"- my heart said silently.

Fight between my mind and my heart started at this juncture only

I had provided her with full sovereignty, whatever she wanted to do she could, I knew only one thing if she really loves me no power in this world could distinct us. If she wanted to stay with me she will, otherwise I never wanted a forceful relationship.

Her b'day was about to knock her door in two days and I hadn't planned anything yet, actually at that time I was out of my pocket so no plans had been executed till then regarding her b'day forecasting, I called one of my friend and borrowed some bucks from him. Now I was in a state to celebrate her day. I called her.

"Hi, what's the plan for tomorrow"- I asked?

"Nothing, I had to go to the college and submit some work to the HOD"- she said

"Is it possible for you to come to Jaipur tomorrow, I need to talk to you"- I asked

"I can come but for a very short period of time, as I had to submit my complete work day after tomorrow"- she said

My mind started making plans for her b'day, one of my cousin was about to come to my place for his exams.

We had planned to celebrate Vinni's b'day together.

She was not aware of any planning made by me and my cousin. It was a total surprise for her.

Very next morning she called me and said that she had boarded her bus and she will come Jaipur in the next three hours. At that time I was surrounded by my dreams and I was in no mood to go anywhere but I had to go, I called my cousin

"Where are you dear? When will you reach Jaipur?" – I asked

"I'm on my way and I will reach Jaipur in two hours"- he said

All were punctual apart from me; I was still lying on my bed and planning to celebrate her b'day. Finally I woke up and started getting ready for her day. When time passed I didn't know, my cell beeped, it was Vinni, I picked up

"I'm about to enter Jaipur, please come fast I hate waiting for you at the bus stand"- she said

I haven't dressed myself up at that time still I said

"I'm on my way to the bus stand and I will reach before you reach the bus stand"- I said confidently

I cut the call and accelerated my dressing speed and left for the bus stand when I reached there she was waiting for me. She was wearing a white color t-shirt and jeans she always used to live simply, she didn't liked make ups and all, I liked her simplicity and her way of living.

"You were about to reach here before I reach, but you are late, I was waiting for you from the last half an hour"- she said angrily.

"I was stuck in traffic that's why I got late, let it be you are looking too pretty"- I said trying to decrease her anger

"Please stop these and tell me why you called me, you said you need to talk to me"- she said

"I will tell you everything, I had called someone and we will clear all the talks in front of him"- I said in a heavy voice.

"Who is coming Vicky? What you need to clear? Everything is clear between us?"

She was panicked, her face turned red, she thought I had called aashu to clear things but my cousin and me had planned a surprise b'day for her, I had saved my cousin number on the name of aashu to panic Vinni. When my cousin called, I intentionally showed my cell to Vinni and she saw the name, she got worried, she was in a condition in which she can't figure out what was happening with her, I picked the call and said him to come to GT as we were also going there, I asked my brother to collect the cake from the bakery as it was ready and settle himself at the place where we were about to come.

The whole journey from bus stand to GT, Vinni was silent she was in a shock what I had done.

I had booked a small hut to celebrate her b'day, my cousin was sitting there waiting for us to arrive, and he was sitting in such a way that when we enter we were not able to see his face. Vinni's step was reducing its covering area as she was moving forward, I asked

"What happened to you? Why are you walking so slowly? See someone is waiting for you" – I said

Vinni stopped and asked me who was sitting there, I asked her to see who was there,

When we finally reached our table and Vinni saw my cousin sitting there, she started hitting me, and said

"Why you were haunting me the whole time? Why have you saved your cousin number with his name?"

My cousin was not able to understand what was happening there between us, he was seeing us in a shocking manner. I consoled my cousin that I will elaborate the full story after her b'day celebration.

"You called me here to celebrate my b'day?"- She said and started blushing

I knew she liked surprises so I planned it; we cut the cake and sang b'day songs for her. She liked chocolates so the cake was full of chocolate syrups and cream.

"I hadn't brought any gifts for you, will it be okay"- I asked

"No, there is a big problem I want my gift right now otherwise I'm not going to give you my b'day cake to eat"- she said and started laughing

I love seeing her smile, she was happy her face was telling all the truth, I asked my cousin to go and get some chocolates for the b'day girl. Actually I wanted to talk to her that's why I sent him, he understood my intentions and nodded his head and went out.

Happy b'day my love, I hugged her and kissed her forehead, her eyes were red, she hadn't imagined I would plan something like that after all that complications and misunderstandings, she broke into tears.

"What had happened to us? Why are we behaving like strangers?"- I asked her

After people, God had also started testing the patience of my love, after a number of failed attempts, they said

"Oh sweet couple you had been approved by us a long time ago we were just checking the spark which you had earlier"

"We don't need any explanation to justify our love, we had the capacity to hear each other silently"- she said

I was happy by her statement and the smile on her face. How was our relationship going on? Full of immaturity, confusion but when it comes to care we never showed our back, we always stand to help each other at our bad times. We loved each other, we both knew that but her innocence was creating problems for our love life.

"No relationship is perfect complications comes with every relation, but we need to strengthen our mind and fight with those complications and make our story perfect"- I consoled her

We had our lunch and I was quite happy about that meeting because I wanted Vinni to feel normal, as she was also in lot of tension about our relation. She had to leave for her college, she always used to come from about 120 km to meet me. I haven't seen any girl doing that much for his love, being a girl she was fulfilling more than enough. When she was about to leave I hugged her and said

"I am sorry I scold you all the time, but I never want to scold you I do so because I don't want to lose you ever. My life depends totally on you" – I said calmly

We were standing at the bus stop waiting for her convenience to arrive, she came close to me and asked me to bring my ears close to her mouth, and I did so

"I don't know how to express my love, I don't know how to express my feelings, and I don't know how to impress you, it doesn't mean that I don't love you, if expressing feelings is called love then I'm ready for this"- she said and boarded her bus.

My cousin was aware of the complications between me and Vinni, as soon as Vinni left he came to me and said

"We need to show that guy his limit, let's meet him and teach him the proper lesson"

"Cool down my boy if I had to teach him the lesson I would have done it very earlier but I don't want that anyone point finger at my girl, I don't want a relationship forcefully. I will get her completely on the basis of my love strength"- I said him

'How could you gather so much of calmness and patience inside you when someone is trying to snatch your girl from you"- he asked

"He can't snatch her, she is not a competition, she is not a child she understands everything better than me, it's her choice which way she wants to go, I have allowed her to fly in the open sky"- I said

"Hats off to your attitude brother, if I had been on your place I could have murdered that guy"- he said

"Fall in love once and you will never talk like this, when you fall in love truly you only want that person to be happy, even if you are not a part of their happiness"- I said

You know one thing all my friends used to say after my fights with her

"Life doesn't stops due to a single person"

I used to say them "My life doesn't starts because of that single person"

We both returned to our place

Chapter 16

Valentine's Day

I was waiting for 14th February our 3rd valentine, we had a ruthless fight and we both were not chattering to each other, this time she was also dogged not to talk to me. I saw the statistics of our anger meter and judged that she was in more anger, so I decided to give her amazement on Valentine's Day.

I called one of her friend and requested her to bring Vinni available on that day, she said that it would be impossible to take her out because from the last few days she had been irritated because of the complications you were going through but I insisted her to try to take her out. I had planned a lot to say sorry to her because I was not able to give her time due to the busy schedule of the college.

I made few cards from my own and purchased few gifts which could bring a smile on her face. I went to her town and asked her friend to bring her to the restaurant where we had decided to celebrate that day. Vinni was not aware of any surprises arranged by me. Her friend asked her to come with her on the name of his boyfriend, I was sitting in the restaurant waiting for them, the road view was clear from that restaurant, I saw Vinni was coming with Mishra, she was dressed like she had come to her college canteen, it wasn't her mistake, she was not knowing that I was about to come, I went to the washroom of the restaurant and left the gifts over the table. Mishra knew that I had arrived to the restaurant but still she was calling me continuously. I stepped out from the washroom and stand behind vinni's chair, Mishra had saw me and she was blushing, as Vinni saw me her face turned red, she hadn't expected that I could be here, she started hitting me with her hand, I hugged her and wished her happy valentine's day. She was shocked, she was not able to speak a single word, and she was just looking at me continuously in disguise.

I handed her all the presents I had got for her, she was blushing after seeing those presents made by me, that valentine I had worked a lot for preparing her gifts. We were very hungry so I asked Vinni to order anything she wanted to eat. She ordered her favorite "masala dosa". I loved her choice and her, I liked to eat from her hands, when she cared for me I felt like the happiest person in the world. She never let me eat with my hands she always used to feed me with her hands.

I was happy seeing her smile she was happy with the surprise I had planned for her. But complications had never left our side.

One of her senior came to that restaurant with his scarce friends, Vinni wished her good afternoon they correspondingly wished the same, they went to the bar of that restaurant. We had finished our meal and we were about to leave, suddenly, those seniors came back, one of them was smoking and he asked Vinni to come outside, I hold vinni's hand and said she will not go anywhere.

They were drunk one of them shouted at me

"If you have the guts then stab to go to your place"

Vinni and his friend started worrying what had happened, Vinni asked me to sit inside and she went to talk to that guy, they started shouting again.

"How he could show me his attitude, I will exterminate him and all Blah! Blah!"

I was listening to them from fairly long time and till then my patience level was at its last point. I went out of the restaurant and asked them to come one on one and if they had to fight with me let the girls go to their residences. Vinni shouted at me and asked me to get inside the restaurant but I was in no mood to tolerate those mini packs.

I asked their master if you hit me here then please don't let me go to my place because once I reached there then I would drag you from your place and hit you very brutally. He was drunk and he was not able to endure my words he moved his hand and his hand touched Vinni's head. I was out of my mind how he could hurt her, I put on an iron rod which was beside me and embattled it on his knees as soon as I hit that rod to him a hockey stick fell on my spinal. Vinni was weeping for the whole time, the restaurant manager called the constabularies, as soon as they came all the guys ran away. Cops enquired what had happened, then the manager told him few drunk guys were disturbing people over there. Police asked me few questions and went away.

Vinni asked me to go to my college as she don't want anything new to be materialize. She and her friend get me a bus and asked me to go.

The guy who hit me was beau of Vinni's friend, while I was on the bus her friend called me

"I'm sorry for his mistakes Vicky, he was drunk that's why he was capable to control his anger. Please don't smash him back. I love him" – she said

"Tell him to fleece as he had hit Vinni on her head and I'm not going to tolerate this, ask him to say sorry to her, otherwise tell him to be ready for the results"- I said and hanged on

Vinni called me after half an hour and said that "he was asking for sorry for what he did".

I said Vinni -"I'm not going to leave him, don't let him emanate to Jaipur otherwise it will be a mess for him".

As I reached Jaipur and told my friends about the happening they became aggressive, they were ready at that time to go to his college drag that guy out and hit him hardly but I stopped them because Vinni was in the same college and it would be a problem for her. I controlled my anger and applied ointments onto the spots of hockey stick area on my back and slept.

Chapter 17

Love, betray

My results were out and I had got a supplementary in my physics paper as expected, I was upset about my failure again I had disappointed my parents but this time I had worked hard but due to the bandages and plasters I was not able to concentrate fully on my studies. I had practiced a lot for the papers but result did not paid the price.

Vinni was out of the town, actually she was at home enjoying her vacations. She was at home from the last one and a half month, I was dying to see her, I missed her so does she. She was about to come to Delhi in three to four days, we had less talks as she was at home and was always being surrounded by different family members.

After a long time we got an opportunity to talk, nobody was there in her room that day. She called me

"Hi baby, how are you"- she said

"I'm fine, when are you coming? My eyes needs to see you please come as soon as possible"- I said

"I'm coming to Delhi in two days after that I had to stay at a friend's place in Delhi and then I will be in Jaipur"- she said

After a long time we had this long duration talk, we were quite excited to meet each other

"Vicky can I ask you something?"- She said

"What happened? Why you need to ask me anything? I trust you"- I said

"Please I have to talk to you regarding this topic, please don't get angry listen to me very calmly"- she said

"Don't jumble the words please tell me what had happened or something which was about to happen"- I said

"Tomorrow I am leaving for Delhi and I had to stay at one of my born friend in Delhi, aashu had called me last night and he was asking me to meet him in Delhi. What should I do?"- She asked me

I was not in the state to answer any of the above questions at that time, I asked her

"What do you want baby? I'm always standing with your decisions. You could go and meet him I have no issues".

"It had been 2 years since we haven't met, we will meet for a short time and then I will come to Jaipur and meet you then we will have lots of fun."- She said consoling me

She was so excited about the meeting, her way of talking had been changed, she was changed, why always me? I asked myself

"Don't ask yourself why someone keeps hurting you? Ask yourself why you are allowing them to hurt you"- My heart said

This time my heart was also shattered, I had permitted her to meet that guy, now I was thinking how I could do that I always used to hurt myself and blame her for the mistakes, before committing any work she always asked me and I was the one who always allowed her to destroy me. It wasn't her mistake she was innocent, I was the main culprit who had still the feeling that she would be mine. How could she would be mine? She had changed. Her way of walking showed that she was on the other path opposite to me.

"I don't have any copyright of your love but I still want to wait for you till my last breathe"- I wanted to say her but I didn't

When I cut the call, I straightly went to my bathroom and slapped myself a number of times in front of the mirror. I hated myself why I allowed her to meet him. Somehow I consoled myself that everything was normal but my heart knew nothing was normal between them. I was burning from inside, I was not able to control my anger.

Sandy came to me and asked "what had happened to you?"

"Please leave me alone, I don't have to explain all of you what's going with me every time"- I said rudely

"Cool down bro I'm just asking because I felt that you were not good. That's it"- he said and went away

Vinni had again provided a reason for me to lose my anger, she knew I hate that guy still she wanted to meet him and she was asking me for the permission letter.

"I'm not a toy madam don't play, I have heart inside"

I thought it was her innocence which was creating a problem in our relationship but it was both of them who were trying to play with me, I called one of my friends in Delhi and asked him to search where aashu was staying in Delhi. I wanted to slap that guy, he was interfering in our happy life. Vinni was blind at that time she was not able to see the pain inside my heart, she was just thinking of her own happiness.

Vinni was on the platform and was waiting for her train she called me

"Hi Vicky, how's you"? – She asked

She was calling me with my name, I was watching her back turning towards me.

"Hi, how's you"? - I said

"I am at the station, I will reach Delhi tomorrow morning"- she said

"Oh good, when is your best friend coming to meet you"- I asked

"He had said that he will be at the junction to receive me"- she said frankly

I had almost lost my girl but still I was trying to drag her back to me, a hard try by my side in favor of my love. She had no guilt about what she was doing, she was happy about their upcoming meeting. I kept aside those thoughts of both of them and went out to my friends to divert my mind from that topic which always provided me with pain. I was sitting silently with them, they found it quite unusual that I was sitting silent, one of them asked me

"What happened bro? Vinni went with some other guy?"- He said

"Shut your mouth otherwise I am going to break it"- I shouted at him and left his room.

My head was about to blast, it was paining quite badly as I reached my place I lied on my bed with tears in my eyes, I was thinking,

"I'm much more when I'm with you, without you I'm nothing"

When my eyes fell I don't know that, when I was up people were shouting at each other, there were 7 people in my room. My whole group was there, they were playing cards and making a lot of noise, I woke up and dressed myself for the college but they didn't let me go, I also sat there and started playing with them, suddenly, my phone rang

"Hi what's up, I have reached Delhi"- She said

Vinni had made my day, somehow I had consoled my heart to swallow that bitter truth and she again filled my empty plate. Why girls don't want men like us to be happy? Whatever she wants to do she can I was not going to stop her but why she let me know those things when I was feeling jealous of that guy.

"Good enjoy with your friend then and don't call me please, I'm busy somewhere with my work"- I said and hanged on

A text message popped on my screen

"Don't you trust me Vicky? If you don't then why you permitted me to go and meet him".

Why should I always understand the situation, can't she understand what I feel inside me, what sort of pain is there inside my heart? I murmured

I asked one of my friends to bring a whole packet of cigarettes as we engineers are expert in turning our anger into the ashes. He brought a whole packet of cigarette, I had never smoked earlier but I had seen people smoking during their bad times that was the worst time for me so I had to, now we were only 4 person left in the room and we all were close to each other and we almost share all the talks between us. They asked me what happened to you why you are so sad but I didn't told them anything. They forced me to tell what had happened to me, finally I told them

You know what is the reason behind my ongoing love story is "whenever she promised me something I trusted her blindly"- I said to them.

After these words my tears were rolling down my face automatically, I was trying to hide them but my friends saw them especially bohra,

Bohra was like a brother to me, he always provided me with the feeling of a brother. We always used to fight on every topic, we never support each other in front of our friends but when it comes to other people, we were the master of them, we don't had fear of anyone in our college or outside the college. We were like the boss in ourselves no one could rule us. He asked me

"What happened to you? Anything serious?"

"Nothing had happened, I had permitted Vinni to meet aashu in Delhi, and now my possessiveness is getting over me and I'm tensed about her"- I said

"Don't you worry she is a sensible girl have trust on your girl"- he said

We were continuously smoking between our talks, he was consoling me "not to worry about her she loves you". I knew she loves me but I knew that bastard he always used to avail the opportunity of her innocence.

I called Vinni but she didn't picked up the call, a message was blinking on my screen

"I'm in metro with aashu, I will call you little later".

I was shocked by her text message, she never stopped me in talking to her she was always ready to talk to me but time changes people. I switched my cell off. I was brooked up I sat down on the floor with a surprised face I was laughing at myself, I was not able to handle the situation, my mind stopped functioning. The only question revolving in my mind was why I allowed her to meet him and I knew the answer, I can't stop her for anything, I want her to be happy, then why was my mind arguing with my heart. We didn't went to the college we smoked almost eighteen cigarettes that day, I was not able to digest the air coming from the cigarettes. We had not eaten a single bite of the food and we were continuously smoking.

When bohra went to his place, I switched my phone on and tried to call her but she didn't picked my call, I tried a number of times but she was so busy with his friend that she was unable to see the pain I was having at that time. I was lying on my bed and thinking about Vinni, how she could ignore me like that

"Life doesn't end when you don't get what you want in your life but there is nothing left in your life when you get what you want and loose it"

I was calling her continuously suddenly she picked up my call.

"Hi where were you I was trying to reach you from a long time, I was getting worried"- I said her

"Why are you behaving like a small kid, I'm safe I am with aashu don't worry I will call you as soon as I reach to my friends place"- she said and hanged on

"I was busy with aashu" oh my god she was saying that to me. My girl was arguing with me on the name of other guy, she was pretending like she was his girlfriend not mine. She had prepared different weapons to let me down in every respect. I didn't knew what I had done to her why she was behaving like that, I had nothing left with me, and all I had was she.

She kept ignoring my calls and messages, I kept burning my soul, and this had only left in our relationship. My relationship was turning towards a different destiny which I never wanted from my point of view. She was proving me wrong, she had made my love feel low, I hated her for that, and she must had some respect for my love.

It was 5'o clock in the evening I called her again still the same answer she was not picking up my phone, I was depressed, I was low I didn't know what was going through my mind, I picked up my compass and started cutting my palm silently as sandy was also sleeping beside me if he came to know about that he would have slapped me, I made lots of cuts on my hand with that compass. My hand was turned red and the floor was totally red, I got up washed my hands with water and went out from the PG. I walked to a medical shop and asked him to bandage my hand, the shopkeeper knew me so he got worried what I had done to myself, he provide me with different antiseptics and bandaged my hand, pain was uncontrollable in my hand, when I reached my hostel sandy was up he saw me and asked what happened to my hands I said nothing just minor cut while playing. I called her again at sharp 9'o clock as she had asked me that she will be at her friend's room. This time she picked in a single ring

"Hi, I have got late because my friend hadn't come to receive me yet she will be here in half an hour"- she said

"You said that you will be at your friend's house till 9, you are alone in that city you must be at your place"- I said angrily

"I'm not a small kid and by the way aashu is with me and he will leave as soon as Shweta arrives"- she said

My care was looking her like a burden, she got irritated by my care, the very first time. Picture had arrived at its climax, all the confusions was getting cleared step by step. Aashu was still with her that late, yes I was a possessive guy, I do care for my girl because I had loved her truly.

"Say thanks to him from my side for looking after you"- I said and hanged on

I was tensed for my girl because she was alone with aashu, I never trusted that guy but she was feeling safe and comfortable with him,

"When you will reach your friend's house please let me know?"- I said

"Oh sure I will surely call you as soon as I reach there."- She said

A single minute on the clock was very hard to pass I was not able to breathe properly, my body was shivering but she was unaware of that, she knew only one thing that she was in a relationship with such a guy who can do anything for me when my tears fall. I had that weak point I can't see her tears, I always wanted her to be happy

It was 10'o clock, I called her again

She didn't picked up. She called me at approximately 11 in the night

"Hi baby, I have reached to shweta's flat, aashu dropped me" – she said

"What should I do if he had dropped you to your friend's flat?"- I said rudely

"Why are you behaving so rude Vicky? Whenever I go out with my friends you start behaving like small kids, you start caring for me a lot. After 3 years I have come to meet

Shweta, what she will think if I would talk to you in front of her"- she said

"I don't know anything please talk to me I need to talk to you, I'm not able to breathe properly. What your friend will think I don't care all I want is to talk to you"- I said

"I will call you in the middle of the night when she will be asleep till then I am turning my phone off, please try and understand I'm sorry"- she said

She never behaved like that in the past 3 years of our relationship, we had faced a number of complications but we never stopped interaction between us but she had switched her phone off due to me. I was feeling quite ashamed that I can't make her happy, why I was not able to understand her situation? She had met her best friend after 3 years, they must need some time to spend together. But she never reacted that way that was a new face of Vinni.

I called her again at 1'o clock, she picked my phone

Hi, is you friend still up? - I asked her

"Yes, actually her friends have come to party with her at her flat, so we are just passing our time, I call you when I am free"- she said

"Boys are allowed at her flat? And you are enjoying the party and don't you even asked a single time what was going inside me"- I said

"This is Delhi and people use to live here together and no one opposes, I am not feeling well due to my journey, I am not enjoying with them, I am having rest in the other room and if you don't believe me then I can't do anything, I knew that you are not well after I had met aashu but I can't change your way of thinking"- she said and switched her phone off

Each and every movement of clock was making my life more and more complicated, I was drowning in my own complicated life. I was feeling ashamed that I had no trust on my love, she can never cheat me. With these thinking I fell asleep. My phone rang at approximately 4'o clock in the morning, it was her

"Hello baby, what was my child doing? Sleeping!! – she said"

"No I can't sleep when you are playing hide and seek with me, why I think you are hiding something from me?"- I said

"I can't hide anything from you, because I don't know how to lie to anyone, whenever I tried I was failed you always caught me"- she said politely

She was returning to her college, I asked her to come to Jaipur as I was willing to meet her but she refused as she was too tired from her journey, she promised me that she will come and meet me before I would go home. My vacation was being started in a week. I called Vinni but she was busy in talking to someone, I called her roommate

"Hi Shruti, where is Vinni and whom she is talking to from the last half an hour"- I said

"Brother, she is busy with aashu and she always used to talk to her in her free times"- she said

"Could you do me a favor, can you get me with the information about them" – I said

"Time had taught me to had eyes on everyone, otherwise I was so straight minded that I trusted everyone blindly"

She was calling me and I was talking to her roommate about her inspection, I was feeling guilty inside me but the situation had made me to do so, I picked her call

"Hi baby, who was on the call?" – She asked me

"It's none of your business, you go and keep yourself busy with your best friend"- I said

"I was talking to my mom as my grandmother had expired last night, and I had to go to my home as soon as possible"- she was sad

"I'm sorry for your loss but how did it happened and how will you go to your home?" – I asked her

"My uncle had arranged the flight tickets and I will be going with him"- she said and hanged on

I wanted to hug her and console her about the situation that had occurred but she had cut the call and she was moving to her house with her uncle, this time I was relaxed about her journey because she was with her family member.

After all the rituals of her grandmother were performed she returned to her college, she asked me to meet her and I was waiting for that time from a long time ago. She came to Jaipur

As usual I was waiting for her at the bus stand, she came to me and hugged me and started crying for her grandmother, I made her feel comfortable and we went again to that native place GT. I asked her if she want to eat something but she denied, she was different, she was not making any eye contacts with me. I was scared what had happened to her, we were quietly sitting together like the strangers, suddenly she broke up the silence

"If I hurt you to your last limit and ask for sorry would you forgive me?" - She asked

"What you think Vinni?"- I cross questioned her

"I know you had a big heart and you will forgive all the mistakes which I had committed"- she said confidently

"She was trying to be in my life again, I thought my prayers had worked but I was wrong she was here for hiding mistakes which she had committed"- my mind said

"What sort of mistakes you are talking about? What had you done? Tell me and I will forgive you"- I said

I haven't done anything which will make our love down, I love you a lot and can't live without you even for a second, and she had changed her mind again, what had happened in Delhi, she had never been so desperate about me.

"Was she really in love with me or she was still fooling me around?"- Fight started between my heart and my mind.

We had our lunch together after a long interval of time, I was waiting her to feed me with her hands but I didn't said that, I tied to pick up my food, she slapped my hand and asked me to sit still as she will make me eat, I was smiling from inside

Whatever changes between us whatever our relation turn out to be but she never stopped caring for me, I was addicted for her care when she was with me, I had missed her a lot during these vacation days. After we completed our lunch she asked me

"Will you forgive any girl cheating his boy?"

"It would depend on the situation, I don't know about different people but if you would be on that place and you had told me your mistakes on your own, and I had the will power to forgive the biggest mistakes of your life" – I said

She was smiling after listening my words.

"How much you love me Vicky?"- She asked

"The only thing I had done in my life perfectly is to love you. I don't know the actual meaning of love but I knew one thing when I see you, I forgot all my pain, my all problems gets its solution, you are like a therapy to me, I can't survive without you" – I said

She hugged me and said sorry for making me feel low, she was sorry for not interacting with me in Delhi when she was with aashu. She had already prepared a base that I can't scold her so was I working according to her setup. She had to leave for her college suddenly her cell rang it was one of her senior, she told me that "one of her senior had stayed with his boyfriend and was not sure about what happened between them as the guy was totally drunk and the girl was not in a condition to handle his guy".

"Why are you telling me these all stuffs?"- I asked her

"She had asked me to bring her a pregnancy kit for her confirmation, please could you buy for her"- she said innocently

"No, why should I do these all things, I don't know that girl and I am not going to buy those rubbish things"- I said

"Please buy it for my sake, otherwise I had to go to the shop and buy it"- she said

I went to the shop and brought what her senior had asked her for, I handed that packet in her hands and asked her to leave as she would be late for her college. Our eyes met but she was not able to make eye contacts with me, we greeted each other bye and moved to our respective places

I was enjoying my vacations at my home, without any tension, I woke up daily at 11, breakfast was ready at the table before I got myself fresh. I was living a royal life according to the engineer point of view, in engineering we had to forget what the meaning of breakfast is. That was the reason when an engineer went to his home, he felt royal.

Vacations were about to end my returning tickets were made by my father the royal life was about to end. One night I was playing games in my cell, a message popped onto my screen

"Hi Vicky, this is Shruti, I need to talk to you"

"Yes, tell sis what happened, how could I help you?"- I said

"Nothing had happened to me I just wanted to talk on vinni's topic"- she said

As I heard that name I started having Goosebumps inside my body. I was shivering with cold or with her talks I didn't knew that.

"You had to stay calm and listen to what I am saying. Please don't panic"- she said

"Please, don't jumble words & tell me what had happened"- I said

"You need to talk to Vinni, she is desperate for that guy, and don't you know what happened in Delhi, I got some chats between Vinni and aashu, and I was not able to digest what was written in those chats"- she said

At that time I was sleeping in my room and my mom and dad were also sleeping beside me I wanted to cry but I wasn't so fortunate to roll down my tears, I was crying inside me, she had proved me wrong again.

"Please send me the screen shots of the chats I want to read it, and please don't tell Vinni ever that I kept a third eye on her"- I said

"I'm not going to send you any of the screenshots; I just want you to stay away from her if you want happiness in your life, otherwise you are free to talk to her"- she said

"I will not take reveal your name in front of her, please send me those screenshots, I want to see the talks between them"- I said

"Let it be there is nothing to see just leave her, she had cheated on you, she don't deserve your love"- she said angrily

"I always thought to heal her wounds and she always brought a new sword to penetrate inside my heart"

She sent me those screen shots and I started downloading it, my heart was pounding heavily, my eyes was not blinking even for a second, I wanted to see the weapon she used to provide me pain. I read their talks, I never believed Vinni cheated on me, I was not believing my eyes I tried to cry but no tears were left in my eyes to fall, I was weeping inside my blanket because my parents were sleeping beside me.

I called Vinni but she didn't picked, I left with a message,

"All wanted us to be separated, I always wanted you to be happy, if you are happy away from me, and I wish I should never be yours."

I was broken by her; it was not her mistake she knew I can't leave without her and that was the point of which she was taking the benefit.

"Why she always used to provide me that pain which I don't deserve? It's because I provided her with the love which she don't deserved"- I said in myself

Vinni called me back.

"What happened baby? What was that message all about?" – She asked innocently

"What were those chats all about? You ignore that message, it's my heart's feeling which is screaming and shouting in pain"- I said politely

"I am not getting what you are talking about, please be clear Vicky"- she said

"What was the Delhi tour all about? Could you explain?" – I asked

"Yes I can explain you everything if you listen to me calmly"- she said

She still wanted me to listen to her with calm, I was in pieces and she wanted me to listen to her excuses. I had heard about girls that they used to be selfish but I hadn't heard they had no feelings for people like us.

"You cheated me, did aashu stayed at your friend's flat? You both were together that night?"- I asked

She was out of her mind, she was completely blank, she was not able to speak a single word and that what she does, she always used to keep mum and let the tears fall but this time I warned her earlier please don't show me your fake tears, because it's like a weapon for you but I always believed in your tears.

"Yes I was with aashu because he was not able to get the last metro, when he left me it was 10.45pm and the last metro was of 11pm, so he was not able to make it to the metro station finally he called me and stayed with us"- she said

"Have you ever tried to understand my feelings, I'm the one who tries to keep you smile the whole day and cries alone the whole night"- I said

"You were together the whole night still you are explaining me with ease". This was the reason you were not picking up my call, you think that I'm a fool that you will say me anything and I could listen to you silently. You know you don't deserve my love you need people who plays with you and your feelings. You can't change Vinni cheating is in your habit and you can't stop that"- I said loudly

"I was feeling sorry for myself that night when you stayed in Delhi, because I thought I was not able to provide full freedom to you. But you ended my whole confusion; you were with my enemy in the same flat under a single roof and in a single room. Wow! Vinni hats off you had provided me with lots of loyalty and love. Why Vinni?" – I asked

"Vicky, the situation was like that when aashu came to drop me at my friend flat, at that time my friend was drinking and when aashu came he also sat with her, I was not able to understand what to do then, they were highly drunk that's why I stopped him and not let him go in that middle night"- she said

Now every question was getting its answers whether her rude behavior, her attitude, her patience and the most important thing that checkup kit which she asked me to buy was not for her senior it was for her, I was shocked, I was crying but no tears came out, my mind was about to blast, I was not in a condition to do anything.

"What happened that night Vinni?"- I asked in anger

"Vicky please try and understand my condition, trust me, I haven't planned for this, I love you, it was a mistake. I tried to tell you the truth but I was not able to gather the strength which needed to tell you the truth. He was drunk he told that he loves me I was not able to get his mentality and when I got that I suddenly called you, he was trying to get over me but he failed, and that kit was just to confirm and nothing else, I wanted to tell you everything that's why I had come to meet you twice but I didn't want to lose you that's why I stopped. Please forgive me Vicky, I'm only yours and you are the only one who can take care of a girl like me"- she said and started crying.

"Go away I don't need you in my life you don't deserve my love, don't dare to call me ever because whatever happened it was all under your consent, so don't teach me I'm not a small kid Vinni, I know you quite well"- I said

"I know I had done a blunder but you should know one thing I loved you, I love you, I will love you forever and no one could stop me"- her voice was breaking

"See Vinni if you love that guy go to him, I will take you to him but spoiling three lives is not a good choice, if that guy is creating problems between us then I must teach him a lesson. Please don't call me from now onwards"- I said and hanged on

She was calling me continuously she knew that she had lost me from her life. She messaged me

"I had cut my veins, if this was the end to our love story then here it is bye Vicky and I'm sorry what I did to you

My phone fell from my hand; I was shocked 'what she had done to herself'. I called her friends and asked them to go to vinni's room as soon as they can, as she had cut her veins.

I called Vinni and said her "to press that cut portion and stop the blood coming out from your body, I have forgotten all the mistakes which you had done, I am only yours, I'm not going to leave you till my last breathe please don't leave me"

I was at my knees before the almighty tears were rolling down my face but I was continuously praying that nothing happen to her, I called her friend she said that we were taking Vinni to hospital as she had cut the main vein and ample amount of blood was out of her body.

I asked my father to book tickets for me as I had to reach Jaipur as soon as I can because my exams date had been shifted. He did so without asking me the appropriate reason.

The whole journey was under the stress, how she would be, why she did that, does she really love me? I was just praying for her wellbeing, suddenly my phone beeped, it was an unknown number, I picked up

"How's Vinni?"- A known voice

"She is fine by the way may I know who's speaking"- I asked

"This is aashu, I just wanted to know how she was"- he asked

"You know you are that kind of termite which compels to burn the furniture, where the furniture had never committed any mistake, you try once calling her and I guarantee I will kill you"- I said and hanged on

I reached Delhi and rushed directly to the hospital, there were few friends of her and she was in the ICU. I was not allowed to go inside and meet her, I was feeling sorry why I scolded her, I sat on the chair and prayed

"I want you to stay with me I want you to fight with me I want you to argue with me, I want your picture inside me, I have heard people saying you love me a lot, please don't leave me"

One of her old friend came rushing to me and said

"Doctor's had asked to bring three units of blood as there are no blood left in their blood bank"

I called one of my friend in Delhi whose father was a renowned doctor in Delhi itself and I asked him to arrange three unit of blood as soon as possible. He asked me to provide all the information regarding the girl and her blood group. I provided him with the same.

Within half an hour we got the required units of blood.

Doctors were busy in making her ready for the operation, she had badly cut her veins and doctors had to operate it and apply stiches on her veins. They were waiting for the blood, I was continuously calling my friend for the blood, he told me that he was stuck in traffic and he is just about to come.

I was continuously in touch with doctors regarding her health. Doctors told me that she had lost a large amount of blood and she needs to be operated as soon as possible.

Suddenly, my friend called me and told me that he was standing near the blood bank at the ground floor of the hospital. I rushed towards the blood bank, I tried with the lift but it was not in work, I rushed towards the stairs and stopped after reaching the blood bank, I took out that slip which had been provided to me for the management of blood and handed it over to the staff which was about to issue blood for Vinni.

I asked him to process his work fast and issue me the blood. I was shouting at him like an insane guy. All people present there were watching me but I just wanted my Vinni to be safe. As he provided me the blood, I again rushed towards the operation theatre and handed the blood units to the nurse and sat on my knees I was tired, my eyes were getting closed by its own.

My friend came after me and helped me in getting up from the floor I had no strength left with me. He let me sat on the chair present over there, I was continuously seeing the bulb outside the operation theatre suddenly it turned on. I was holding my hands together and I was praying to god for her recovery.

"She is struggling there because of me"- I said to my friend beside me.

"What are you saying?"- he asked

"I had scolded her and she made cuts on her hand."- I said him and slapped myself.

Suddenly the lights turned off and I stood up and rushed towards the gate, after few minute doctors came out

"She is out of danger you could meet him"- doctor said to me

I hold doctor's hand and thanked him for her recovery, I stepped my steps forward to her at the ICU to meet her, there were a number of friends of her came to meet her, when I reached there I was not able to see vinni's face it was hidden by her friends, somehow I managed to see her down face, she hadn't saw me till then, I saw the bandage on her hand, she was wearing an oxygen mask which was preventing her to speak.

She saw me and tried to get up but I stopped her, she tried to remove her mask and talk to me but i stopped her this time again. I told her

"Rules are needed to live life but rules are not more important than you"

Sorry was blinking in her eyes; she was not able to make eye contact with me, I went close, kissed her forehead and said

"We are made for each other"

"Doctor have called you he wanted to talk to you"- one of the attendants informed me

"I asked Vinni to have rest as I am coming after meeting the doctor". She nodded her head as the mask was preventing her to speak. I reached and knocked the cabin of the doctor. He asked me to come in as he was waiting for me. I was scared, my fingers were crossed, I was trembling in front of the doctor. He asked me to settle down myself. I sat on the chair in front of me

"Who are you? Why are you getting worried for that girl so much?"

"Sir I can't tell you who am I but I can't see her in pain, she had cut her veins due to my words.

"Please don't let her feel any burden on her body as she had lost ample amount of blood"- doctor said

"Is she alright doctor?"- I asked him

"Yeah she is out of danger we had provided her with proper amount of blood"- doctor said

"Thank you doctor thank you very much"- I thanked the doctor and left his cabin

I was in a dilemma where my mind and heart was saying two different things. I was confused with my relationship status, I accused god why he indulged me in such a situation where I had to make a tough decision which makes my heart shattered into pieces.

"Why always I had to make the decisions?"- my mind lampooned

I wanted her to be graceful and safe and nothing more than that, I wanted her to be happy in her life, I wanted to fulfill all her dreams. I loved her.

Printed in the United States
By Bookmasters